JEREMIAH STOKELY

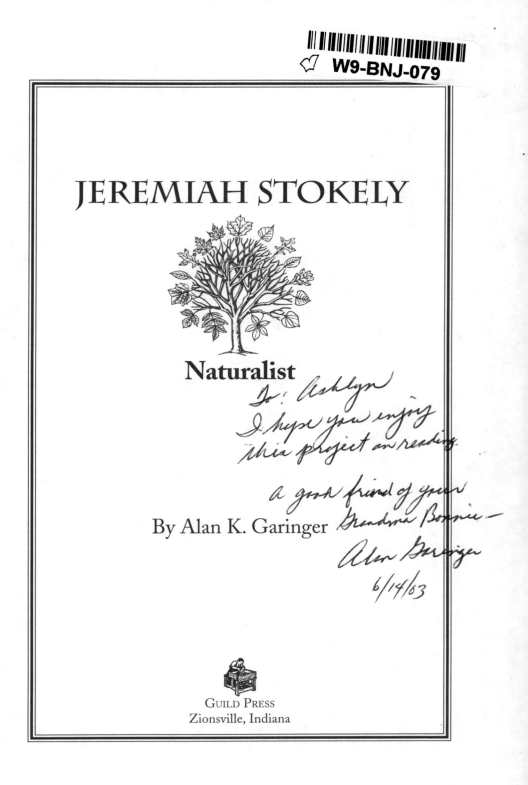

Naturalist

To: Ashlyn
I hope you enjoy
this project on reading.

a good friend of your
Grandma Bonnie —
Alan Garinger
6/14/03

By Alan K. Garinger

GUILD PRESS
Zionsville, Indiana

JEREMIAH STOKELY
NATURALIST

GUILD PRESS
10665 Andrade Drive
Zionsville, Indiana 46077

The Guild Press website address is
www.guildpress.com

ISBN 1-57860-132-0
Library of Congress Catalog Card Number 2003102505

Text and layout design by April Altman Reynolds
Cover design and illustrations by Ronald E. Groves

Printed and bound in the United States of America

FOR PAT AND PETE

Dreams

Hold fast to dreams;
for if dreams die,
life is a broken–winged bird
that cannot fly.

Hold fast to dreams;
for when dreams go,
life is a barren field
frozen with snow.[1]

— Langston Hughes

[1] From THE COLLECTED POEMS OF LANGSTON HUGHES by Langston Hughes, copyright © 1994 by The Estate of Langston Hughes. Used by permission of Alfred A. Knopf, a division of Random House, Inc.

CHAPTER ONE

Jeremiah Stokely slouched on his front porch. He picked aimlessly at a splinter on the worn top step. A yellow moving van pulled into the drive of the Johnson house across the street. He hated moving vans. On the other side of town, a similar truck was arriving at Todd's house to swallow the Miller family's belongings.

This was the first day of summer vacation. But tomorrow, Todd would be gone—Todd, his best friend, with whom he had shared everything since second grade and birthdays since the day they were born. Todd would miss their very first adventure, a trip to see the wild animals at Rescue House.

"Jeremiah," his mother called. "Come and set up the TV trays in the living room. Todd will be here in a few minutes."

"Okay, Mom." He didn't move.

Jeremiah had known something was wrong when Todd's father had dropped Todd off in the top of the second inning of their first Little League game of the season. Todd shuffled into the dugout and slammed his mitt onto the bat bag. Instead of their usual happy sparkle, his black eyes snapped with anger.

"We're moving to Angola. Dad's been transferred," Todd had said.

"Come on, Jeremiah," his mother called again. Nina Stokely had taken the afternoon off from her job at Mason's Supermarket. She stood in the doorway holding a broom, a dust cloth and a can of dusting spray. A dark curl stuck to the perspiration on her neck. She had cleaned the house and made ham salad sandwiches. Todd was to sleep over on his last night in East Newport.

Jeremiah stood reluctantly, then finally pulled at the sagging screen door, but it stuck at the bottom. He yanked and it sprung open and struck him, raising a red welt just below his right eye.

"Dammit!" he shouted.

"Jeremiah Stokely, I don't ever want to hear you say that again!"

"Bill says it."

"You're not Bill. I mean it, now."

"But it hurt, Mom."

"I don't care. You're not to use such words. Hear me?" She turned away quickly, but not before Jeremiah saw the angry set of her jaw.

Jeremiah's shoulders sagged and he stared at the decaying porch floor.

"Let me see." His mother pulled off his Cincinnati Reds cap, pushed back the shock of blond hair and examined the injury. "The skin's not broken," she said gruffly. "You'll live. Go wash your face and set up the trays."

Jeremiah inspected the damage in the mirror. *How come Mom's such a grouch today? She didn't have to yell just because I said a bad word. It wasn't that bad of a word anyway. Packleruma!* He thought. "Packleruma!" he said aloud. Then he smiled ever so slightly. His mind took him back to the first day he, Todd and Stacy Hunter ever said that word. Miguel Sanchez had said something in Spanish on the playground, and Rebecca Smoot, the snitch, told their teacher that Miggy was saying bad words.

"What did he say?" their teacher had asked.

"I don't speak Spanish," Rebecca had said.

"Well, what did it sound like?"

"It sounded like 'packleruma,' but I know it was bad," Rebecca had replied.

Jeremiah, Todd and Stacy had overheard all this. They thought it was so funny that "packleruma" became their universal bad word.

He moistened a washcloth with cold water and gingerly touched the welt. It didn't hurt much. Other times he might have ignored it, but today he was feeling sorry for himself—every part of himself. He draped the cloth over the faucet and went to the kitchen.

Jeremiah smelled chocolate chip cookies. His mother had just taken them out of the oven. They were Todd's all-time favorite food. The table where he and Todd had shared countless cookies and glasses of milk was littered with photography textbooks, photographs and notes from his mother's night class at Community College. The camera she had borrowed from the college library was perched precariously atop the clutter. He pushed aside one of the books and glanced at the newest set of pictures his mother had taken.

"I'm just sorting out the shots I want to have evaluated in class tonight," Nina said.

He set two tray tables in front of the battered couch. When he heard the Millers' van stop in front of the house, he looked out the door. Behind the van, Todd struggled with a large cardboard box. He motioned to Jeremiah to come help him.

Jeremiah took off in a dead run toward the van.

"What's in it?" Jeremiah asked, lifting a box flap.

"Junk I'm not going to move. I know how much you like junk. I can't carry it by myself."

"Todd," Mrs. Miller called from the cab. "I'll pick you up at nine in the morning. Please behave yourself. Nina, make him behave."

Nina waved and nodded from the doorway.

The heavy box flopped awkwardly as the two boys stumbled with it toward the house. They groaned as they wrestled it up the porch steps.

"What have you guys got there?" Nina peered through the loose screen of the door.

"Hi, Mrs. Stokely. Stuff I'm not taking with me."

"Come on in and eat. You can carry the box up to your room later, Jeremiah. Is there enough space somewhere in that horrible mess for one more box?"

The boys sank into the couch and started eating. When Nina returned to the kitchen, Todd whispered, "I've got this great idea. My parents are so sick of hearing me complain about moving they won't even let me talk about it. I think we should do something to protest."

"Like what?

"Why don't we shave our heads?"

"Shave our heads? Are you crazy?"

"No, I'm mad. If we shaved our heads, every time they looked at us they'd know we were mad, and we wouldn't have to say a word. They can't yell at us for complaining if we're not saying anything."

"No way, I'm not cutting off my hair, Todd."

"Let's get a tattoo, then."

"Tattoo? That's the worst idea you ever had. Besides, where could we get a tattoo?"

"We could sneak out to the tattoo parlor behind the record shop on Vine Street."

"I'm not even listening to you. Get a tattoo?" Jeremiah put his hand on Todd's forehead to check his temperature.

"What's this about a tattoo?" Nina said as she returned with a carton of milk to refill their glasses.

"Todd thinks he can get back at his parents by getting a tattoo. He says it's a protest. Tell him he's crazy, Mom."

"You're crazy, Todd."

Todd suddenly became more serious than Jeremiah had ever seen him. He looked at Jeremiah and then at Nina.

"I know it's crazy, but if I don't think crazy thoughts, I'm afraid—"

Todd turned away and looked at the wall. Nina put her hand on his shoulder. Through his bravado, she could see tears starting to fill his eyes.

"We're going to miss you, Todd. But it isn't like you're going to Katmandu. Angola is only a hundred miles away."

"A hundred and twelve," Todd said in a small voice.

"Okay, a hundred and twelve. But, your mother said you can come here for a week and Jeremiah can go there for a week. It isn't like we won't ever see you again." Nina bent to look into his dark eyes, but Todd wiped his face on his sleeve and turned away.

"I'll write you every week, Jeremiah."

"Todd, you don't write letters," Jeremiah said with a laugh.

"I do, too."

"The only letter you ever wrote was when we were in Mrs. Pulaski's third grade."

"Not true," Todd protested.

Jeremiah laughed. "It's true, Mom. We were supposed to be learning to write friendly letters. We were writing to kids in the other third grade and Todd wrote a letter to Timmy Slade."

"You tell everything you know, don't you," Todd said. He tried to put his hand over Jeremiah's mouth, but Jeremiah ducked.

"Listen, Mom, this is good. Todd's letter said, 'Dear Timmy, When I see you on the playground, I'm going to beat you up. Your friend, Todd.' Some friendly letter."

"I got an A-plus on that letter, smart guy."

"Only because Mrs. Pulaski thought Timmy deserved to be beat up."

Todd grabbed Jeremiah around the neck. He put all his force into a headlock, and they rolled in a laughing tangle to the floor.

Nina moved the trays out of the way. Normally, she wouldn't have allowed roughhousing in the living room, but these were not normal circumstances.

The boys lay on the floor, out of breath. They propped their heads against the tattered couch and shoved the last two cookies into their mouths.

Nina organized her schoolwork, placed the borrowed camera in a canvas bag and came to the door of the living room. "I'm going to class now. I'll be back in about two hours. Todd, don't get a tattoo while I'm gone."

"Tell him not to shave his head either, Mom," Jeremiah said.

"Todd, don't shave your head."

"Okay, Mrs. Stokely. Can I pierce my nose and put a ring in it?"

"Please don't do anything weird. See you guys after a while."

She kissed her fingertips and patted both boys on the cheek, picked up her canvas bag and started for the front door.

"You'd better get this box to your room, Jeremiah," Nina said.

"Okay, Mom. See ya."

They struggled with the box of Todd's junk until they got it to the top of the stairs. Jeremiah shoved over a knee-high stack of old *National Geographic* magazines so they could maneuver the box into his room.

Out of breath and wiping perspiration, they sat on the edge of Jeremiah's bed.

"I see that Bill Loker is still giving you old *National Geographic*s," Todd said.

"I bet I have the best collection in town," Jeremiah bragged.

"Do you read them?"

"Of course, stupid."

"Just asking. Packleruma!"

Jeremiah picked up a four-foot-long redwood sign with the carved inscription, "Why are you NOT in here?"

"You like this sign Bill made for me?"

"What does it mean?" Todd asked.

"It's from one of Bill's favorite stories. There were these two friends, poets or something, a long time ago. One was Henry and the other was Waldo."

"I used to have a book about a Waldo who wore a red striped shirt and got lost in crowds. Is that the one?"

"No, Todd, these guys were real and lived a long time ago. Henry didn't think his taxes should be used to buy guns for war, so he wouldn't pay them. They threw him in jail."

"How much did he owe?"

"A dollar and a quarter."

"He went to jail for a dollar and a quarter?"

"It's not the amount. It's the principle. Anyway, that's what Bill says."

"So what's the rest of the story?"

"Well, Waldo went to visit Henry in jail. He said, 'Henry, why are you in here?' and Henry said, 'Waldo, why are you *not* in here?'"

"Well, that's dumb; he wasn't in there because *he* paid *his* taxes."

"That's not the point, Todd. Henry went to jail for something he believed. He thought Waldo should have done the same. It was a protest."

"For a dumb dollar and a quarter? I have to move and you won't let *me* protest?"

"Get a life, Todd."

"Want to see the junk I brought?" Todd asked. He jumped off the bed, opened the flaps of the box, and ceremoniously withdrew a ball glove.

"Ta-daaa. My old mitt. You'll have more use for this than I will."

"Won't you need it in Angola?"

"I've got my new mitt broken in."

Todd dug into the box again. This time he pulled out his rollerblades.

"You can *have* the mitt, but I'm just loaning you the blades. Hey, remember the first time we used them on the parking lot of the church?"

"Cool, thanks, Todd." Jeremiah remembered well the afternoon at the Baptist Church parking lot.

Jeremiah pulled a handful of newspaper clippings from Todd's box. "What's this stuff?"

"Articles Mom cut out of the paper. I was afraid they'd get lost before we got to our new house."

They leafed through the clippings.

"Hey, here's the picture of our tee-ball team the year we played in Richmond. That was the first year that boys and girls played on the same teams," Jeremiah said.

"Look at Brad doing that silly rabbit-ear thing behind your head. He's such a jerk. Do you think he'll be your best friend now?"

"You'll always be my best friend, no matter where you live. Brad's being real nice, though. I guess he's trying to make up for all the trouble he got me into. Maybe he's learned his lesson."

They looked at each other. "No way!" they both shouted.

"There's Stacy at bat. Look how short her hair is," Todd laughed.

"Look how short *she* is," Jeremiah said. "I can't believe it. This picture was taken just three summers ago. She was shorter than I was then. Now she's more than an inch taller than me."

"Girls grow different than boys."

"No fooling," Jeremiah said, remembering how grown-up Stacy had become.

Todd continued to drag things out of the box.

"A boom-box with tape *and* CD player? And earphones? Are you sure you want to leave these?" Jeremiah said.

"Got another one just like it for my birthday. Lots of CDs in here, too." He showed Jeremiah several iridescent disks.

They poked through the box and found Todd's old Junior Detective set with real handcuffs, a badge and a fingerprint kit. The tattered box disintegrated in Todd's hands, spilling the contents on the floor. Jeremiah picked up the handcuffs and hung them on the doorknob. They remembered when they both pretended they were detectives and set out to solve all the crimes in East Newport, even though there were no crimes to be solved.

There were jigsaw puzzles and a dog-eared deck of UNO cards, a box of sixty-four broken crayons and a handful of scented felt markers. They found an envelope with Todd's old report cards.

"Don't you think your mom might want these? I know my mom keeps mine," Jeremiah said.

"I took out the good ones for her."

They leafed through some more clippings and spent the usual amount of time arguing about almost every one of them.

They were so engrossed that they were surprised to hear the front door slam.

"I brought burgers and fries. Anybody interested?" Nina called.

After a race down the stairs, they cleared the table, ate the burgers and played "remember when." They had done that a lot lately.

Nina glanced at the clock. "Nearly nine-thirty. I suppose it would be too much to ask that you guys get a good night's rest."

"You think we're going to stay up all night, don't you, Mom?" Jeremiah said as they headed for the stairs.

"You did the last time Todd was here. I'm telling you guys, the giggling stops at eleven o'clock. I've got to go to work early tomorrow."

It made no difference that they had promised Nina they wouldn't keep her awake. The deadline came and went and the laughter continued. It was after midnight when exhaustion ultimately won.

CHAPTER TWO

Jeremiah's moment of dread came at nine-thirty the next morning. He had wondered how he would say goodbye to his best friend. But when Mrs. Miller pulled up in front of Jeremiah's house, the two friends gave each other a high-five, said "see ya" and then Todd was gone.

All of the sadness Jeremiah had been expecting wasn't there. They had worked that all out last night. Other times Todd had stayed the night, they had played a delaying game, finding one excuse after another to stay just a little longer. They didn't do that this time. Bill had told Jeremiah once that friendship was the first cosmic traveler because it didn't rely on time or space. Now Jeremiah knew what he meant.

Jeremiah trudged back to the house. In the kitchen, a strawberry magnet held a note on the refrigerator:

Jeremiah, Don't forget. Officer Willig is coming at 10:30 to take you to see the animals at Rescue House.

How could he forget that? This was the first of the summer's adventures that he and Todd had set up. The rest of the note was news to him.

Guess what? Just found out your next year's English teacher moved into the Johnson house. What do you think of that? Clean your room, okay? Be good. Love you.

"Yessss!" Jeremiah said, pumping one arm.

Jeremiah wasn't so excited about having his English teacher live in the neighborhood, but her son Joseph was another matter. Joseph Fowler was the most popular student at East Newport High. He was the quarterback of the football team, forward on the basketball team, president of the junior class, and captain of the debate team that won national honors. His picture was in the newspaper all the time.

Jeremiah felt lucky to have a celebrity living on his block. He began plotting ways to get to know Joseph better.

He went to his room. He smiled when he saw the heap of Todd's "junk" on the floor. It reminded him of all the laughter of the night before.

He thought of Rescue House. For six weeks, Jeremiah had been looking forward to seeing how they take care of injured wild animals.

He picked up his dirty clothes and plucked a sock from the lamp shade. Jeremiah hated cleaning his room. Every time he did it, he lost things that took him days to find. He picked up the book Bill had given him for his birthday. It was about safety in operating power tools, something he really wanted to know. He put it on a shelf and hung the safety goggles that came with it over the edge of the mirror. His mom had given him a journal book for his birthday. It had blank pages to write in. He squeezed it onto another shelf.

He started to sort through his pile of new treasures that Todd had given him. He pulled out the rollerblades.

"Cool!" he exclaimed. He had time to kill before Charlie Willig, the conservation officer, arrived to take him to Rescue House. He grabbed the skates and ran out of the house. Maybe if he were skating on the church parking lot right across the street from Joseph Fowler's house, he might "accidentally" get to see his idol.

As he sat on the curb and put on the skates, he looked toward Joseph's house, but saw no one.

In a few minutes, Joseph drove into the Fowler driveway. Jeremiah pretended not to notice. He made a fast circle in the parking lot just as Joseph got out of the van.

"Hey, Jeremiah. I guess we're neighbors now," Joseph shouted.

Jeremiah stopped at the curb. "Hi, Joseph. Guess so."

Joseph ambled across the street to where Jeremiah stood. Joseph was much taller than Jeremiah had thought.

"Cool skates, man."

"They belong to my friend Todd. He moved and I'm keeping them for him."

"You ought to have knee-pads and a helmet."

"I'm not doing anything fancy," Jeremiah said. He felt his ear lobes tingle—the first sign that he was going to blush and ruin this all-important "chance" meeting. His own voice pounded in his ear. *Stupid, stupid, stupid! You should have worn the pads and helmet.*

"Doesn't matter how careful you are. You shouldn't skate without pads and helmet. How'd you get the black eye?"

"I hit myself with a door."

Joseph laughed. "Come on, man. That's the oldest story in the world. What really happened?"

"No kidding. I really hit myself with the screen door."

"Well, black *eyes* are cool. Look at me. I'm black all over."

Jeremiah wasn't sure how to respond. He didn't like comments about people's color. They made him uncomfortable even if they came from a black person. He didn't know where to look.

Joseph sensed Jeremiah's uneasiness. "Just kidding, man," he said. "I went back to our old house for a basketball. I haven't tried out the goal behind the garage here. Want to do a little one-on-one?"

Joseph Fowler asking me to play one-on-one? I can't believe it. Jeremiah was so flattered that he stammered. "I'm . . . I'm not very good at basketball. I'm . . . too short."

"Being tall isn't everything. Speed is just as important. I know you're fast. You'd make a good guard. I was a timer at the elementary track meet last fall. You won every race you were in."

Jeremiah grinned and tried not to look too pleased that Joseph had remembered him.

"Come on over. Let's shoot a few hoops before you fall off those things and mess up your brain."

Joseph waited as Jeremiah took off the blades and tied his ragged shoes. Jeremiah couldn't help comparing their shoes. His were Taiwan replicas of designer sneakers. Joseph's were the real thing.

Jeremiah tied the purple strings of the blades together, slung them over his shoulder and followed Joseph across the street.

"Seen Mr. Loker lately?" Joseph asked. He retrieved the ball from the back of the station wagon.

"Yeah, about every day. He's like a part of our family."

They walked around the garage to a paved court painted like a real basketball court.

"My dad thinks he's one of the great men of the century," Joseph said as he sank a fifteen-footer that hit nothing but net.

Jeremiah ran to get the rebound. "How come?"

"They've been friends since graduate school." Joseph faked left, then turned right around Jeremiah and sank a lay-up.

"What's graduate school?"

"That's where you go to get a doctorate degree, kid."

"I didn't even know Bill went to college," Jeremiah said in a surprised voice."

"Mr. Loker is super-educated. Used to be a college professor."

"Bill never told me that."

"My dad met him in Louisiana. We moved to East Newport because Mr. Loker lives here. Keep your knees bent and your hands low when you guard someone. Keep them high when they're going to shoot."

Jeremiah knew Arthur Fowler, Joseph's dad. He was a professor at the local university and often came to Bill's antique shop to visit.

But how come Bill never told me about Louisiana? Jeremiah wondered.

The two boys, one tall and one short, played one-on-one and had a free-throw contest, both of which Jeremiah lost. Joseph was awesome.

After another game of one-on-one, Joseph said he had to get busy before his mother yelled at him. Jeremiah was surprised that Joseph would say that. He knew Joseph's mother. She was the kindest, quietest teacher he had ever known.

"I guess I'll see ya around," Joseph said and waved goodbye.

As Jeremiah ran back to his house, he felt taller already.

◈ ◈ ◈

Jeremiah was sitting on the front porch when a tan pickup truck, with a big green "DNR" and the Indiana State Department of Natural Resources, seal stopped at the curb. Officer Charles Willig was at the wheel.

Charlie motioned for him to get in. In the short time Jeremiah had known him, the conservation officer had become a good friend.

"Well, Jeremiah, how'd you get the black eye?" Charlie asked.

"Is it really black?" Jeremiah strained to look at himself in the rearview mirror.

"I've seen worse," Charlie said with a smile in his voice.

"I hit myself in the face with a door. I really did."

"Yeah, right." Charlie laughed out loud. He turned the truck around and headed north. "Well, Jeremiah, we have a big surprise for you."

"What's that?"

"Rita has several animals ready to take back to the wild. She's the vet at Rescue House, and she said you could go along."

They drove to Rangeline Road and turned west. Jeremiah didn't get outside of East Newport much. Sometimes Bill took him and his mother to Indianapolis. He used to go with Todd's family to a Cincinnati Reds game once a year. Before his dad left, they went to Ohio or Michigan on summer vacations. But now he was usually no more than bicycle distance from home.

"How far is Rescue House?" Jeremiah asked.

"Not far. You'll like Rita. She has a remarkable way with animals, especially birds. She's also an artist."

They turned down a gravel road and through a gate in a split rail fence. There was a sign that said "Chipmunk Crossing." The road wound around a wooded hill, crossed a stream and ended at a large log building surrounded by screen-wire pens.

A slim, dark-haired woman in a white lab coat met them at the door. She had strong, slender fingers with nails closely trimmed and scrubbed. Her hands reminded Jeremiah of his doctor's hands.

"Rita Cuzak, I'd like you to meet my friend Jeremiah Stokely. You have a lot in common," Charlie said.

She held out her hand. "Jeremiah, I'm so glad to finally meet you."

Jeremiah shook her hand. The corners of her jet-black eyes

crinkled as she smiled. Her dark hair hung down her back in a single, large braid.

"I'm glad you can go with us today. I have someone over here who wants to see you."

She led him around a stack of metal cages and opened a door to a room that was completely walled with glass.

"You can start loading up, Charlie," Rita called. She motioned for Jeremiah to come closer. "Look who's in here." Rita lifted a wire cage so that Jeremiah could see the small owl inside.

"Spot!" Jeremiah shouted. Here was the little owl he had rescued just a few weeks ago.

"It's time to get your little friend back to the woods," she said, handing the cage to Jeremiah. "I never heard the whole story about how your owl ended up here."

"He was tangled in some bushes at the library and a cat was prowling around. He was hurt pretty bad, so I took him home."

"Her, you mean. It's a female screech owl," Rita corrected. "And that's how you met Charlie? He thinks a great deal of you and your mother."

"Well, actually, what happened is Brad Sanders, a friend of mine, got mad at me and turned me in for keeping Spot in a cage. Charlie came and arrested me."

"Arrested you? I don't believe that for a minute."

"He did, sort of. That's when he brought Spot here."

"You made quite an impression on Charlie. He talks about you all the time. Looks like everything worked out. You saved a bird and gained a new friend."

"Yeah." Jeremiah saw how tenderly she looked at the owl. Spot had caused him to meet Charlie. Now, because of the owl, Jeremiah had met another kindred spirit. "Where do you take the animals to let them go?"

"Today we're taking them to the Sink."

"Where's that?"

"It's a wetland area just outside of town. Here, Jeremiah," Rita said. "You take Spot and we'll go help Charlie finish loading."

They loaded two cages that held young opossums. Another one

held a mother opossum with babies clinging to her back. A larger cage contained a hysterical fox, and the rest held rabbits. Jeremiah carried Spot.

Charlie clanked the tailgate shut and they climbed into the cab. Jeremiah held the door for Rita and took the seat by the window.

They went south on Broadway and turned the corner. Jeremiah saw Stacy sitting in a lawn chair at her grandmother's beauty shop. He couldn't resist calling to her.

He rolled down the window and waved. "Hey, Stacy," he shouted.

Stacy waved, and Jeremiah could see in the side mirror that she watched until they turned the corner onto Jackson.

"Someone you know, Jeremiah?" Charlie asked.

"Stacy Hunter. She's in my class at school."

Charlie pointed toward the east. "The Sink is about two miles from here."

Jeremiah was surprised that he didn't know about a wild place for animals so close to home. He had explored East Newport and the nearby countryside on his bike and prided himself on knowing where everything was.

"Why is it called the Sink?"

"When the glaciers were here, they scooped out deep ravines," Rita said. "The wetland we call the Sink was part of that ancient drainage system."

Charlie turned the truck onto a rutted gravel road. "It's still unstable and the ground sinks."

"Sinks? Is it dangerous?" Jeremiah asked.

Charlie laughed. "Only if you stay too long."

"It only sinks a couple inches a year," Rita said.

"How come I didn't know about this place?" Jeremiah asked.

"It's hard to get to. We'll go down the abandoned railroad bed to Hog Creek and walk the last quarter-mile."

They bumped along the ridge of the old rail path that was much higher than the land around. It was like driving on a highway through the tops of the trees. They were only a short distance from where they had seen Stacy. Already it seemed they were miles away from civilization.

Charlie stopped the truck on an old railroad bridge. The steep railroad bed slanted down several feet to the edge of Hog Creek. The sides were covered with spring flowers—spring beauties, violets and a lot of other blooms that Jeremiah didn't recognize.

"This is about as close as I can drive," Charlie said.

Just then they saw a car parked on the other side of the bridge. Two men were taking turns looking at Hog Creek through a surveyor's instrument.

Charlie made a hopeless gesture with his hands. "What now?" he said. "Rita, you and Jeremiah start carrying the cages down. I want to see what these guys are up to."

Jeremiah retrieved Spot's cage and one containing a rabbit. Rita picked up the remaining rabbit cages. They slid down the ridge and scrambled through the undergrowth along the stream.

At the base of the railway embankment stood an enormous sycamore tree that slanted out over Hog Creek. Its branches were so low that they could barely get the cages past the tree. Jeremiah was glad when Rita put down her cages to rest. It signaled that he could do the same.

"Let's rest a minute," she said. She leaned against the trunk of the huge sycamore.

The undergrowth was so dense that they could barely see Charlie, but Jeremiah heard muffled sounds that told him Charlie was having an intense argument with the men on the bridge.

They had made another trip to the truck before Charlie finally arrived carrying the rest of the cages.

"Idiots!" he said. "The county wants to dredge Hog Creek. It would destroy all of this if they did. If I can't get the state to take it over quickly, all this will be lost."

Jeremiah followed Charlie and Rita into the woods. They had walked only a few yards when Jeremiah realized what a marvelous place this was. It didn't look like Indiana. It was just like pictures of a Louisiana bayou in one of his favorite *National Geographic* magazines. A hazy mist clung to the water that spilled over the edge of the creek into a shallow lake. Channels disappeared between gray-green islands. The distant sound of a farm tractor echoed hypnotically through the ravine and hummed in Jeremiah's ears.

In that instant, his imagination took him to a Louisiana bayou.

He and his mother sped through the misty swamp on an airboat. Spanish moss whipped by them as his mother took one picture after another with the expensive camera that he had bought for her.

"Let me put Spot in the boat," Charlie said.

Jeremiah was jarred from his daydream. The sultry Louisiana breeze stopped. The Spanish moss swaying from the cypress trees was replaced by wild grapevines draped from cottonwoods. And the airboat became a small rowboat in a tiny wetland just east of town.

"We'll take them all to the hill. If we leave the fox here, the rabbits will have a chance of getting away before the fox finds them," Rita said.

Jeremiah stopped in his tracks. "You mean you're going to leave the rabbits here even though the fox might kill them?"

"The hill is about a quarter of a mile away. This time of year it's surrounded by water like a little island. The bunnies can live there until the spring rains stop and the water drains. By then Mr. Fox may have wandered off to other places," she explained.

"What if he doesn't wander off?" Jeremiah asked.

"Foxes eat rabbits, Jeremiah. That's the way nature works."

Jeremiah looked wistfully at the rabbits in the cages. She was right, of course. Foxes do eat rabbits in general. *But when you know the rabbits personally,* he thought, *it's a different story.*

They put on life jackets and launched their small craft into Hog Creek. Charlie handed Jeremiah the oars.

Soon they were out of the creek and in a shallow lake. It was a magic land where cottonwoods and sycamores stood in shallow, mirror-like water. Jeremiah noticed teeth marks in the trees at the water line.

"Are there beavers in here?"

"A large community," Rita told him. She pointed to the south. "The dam is over there. That's one of the reasons all this water is here."

"And another reason for not dredging the creek," Charlie said.

"How are you coming on your project to turn the Sink into a

state park?" Rita asked Charlie.

"I have my proposal about done. I need to get some photographs of the area to put with it. A proposal is just words, but with photographs, it's a *presentation*."

"Mom's a photographer. Maybe she'd do it for you," Jeremiah said.

"That's a good idea, Jeremiah. Why didn't I think of that? I'll ask her," Charlie said.

Charlie pointed to a hill covered with small willows and mulberry trees standing just a few feet above the water. At the highest point, the remains of a farm building squatted among the trees.

As they approached, Charlie motioned for them to be still.

"Look," he whispered. "An Eastern bluebird! That's the first one I've ever seen here."

"That's a good omen," Rita said. "It's my namesake."

Before Jeremiah could ask what she meant, the bird flitted off into the bushes. They landed the boat at the base of the island. They struggled through undergrowth to move the cages to an open space near the crest of the hill.

Rita opened each cage and motioned to Charlie and Jeremiah to move back. They watched from the bushes a few feet away. The rabbits were the first to leave. Soon the opossums waddled out of their cages and into their rightful world. Jeremiah was still carrying Spot.

"Okay, Jeremiah. It's time to see if Spot is ready to leave us. Put the cage out there, open the door, and come back here where she can't see you," Rita told him.

He followed her instructions. Spot made a small clucking sound as the cage opened. Jeremiah returned to his friends, but Spot didn't leave the cage.

"We'll just sit here and wait a little," Rita whispered. "The cage still feels like home to her." The only sounds were the wind in the trees and the chattering of squirrels.

"We simply must restore this place to the way it was," Charlie whispered.

"I've told you about the seven generations but you won't listen," Rita said.

"Now don't get radical on us, Rita. It has come a long way. The bluebird is evidence of that," Charlie said.

Jeremiah didn't understand what Rita meant about "seven generations" or what Charlie meant about Rita being "radical."

"But so much has been lost," Rita said wistfully. "Think of all the animals and birds that were here when the white settlers came."

"But they're starting to come back. Even bluebirds would return if we had a bunch of bird houses down here," Charlie said. "That's why the state wants to turn this into a nature preserve. The funds are available. And all the owners have agreed to sell the land. Can you believe the county wants to drain it?" He turned. "Hey, look—Spot's leaving the cage."

Spot waddled out. She looked first one way, then the other. She opened her long-unused wings to test the breeze, and in an instant she swooped over their heads. She perched in a mulberry tree and blinked at them.

Jeremiah felt like cheering but he just whispered, "Goodbye, Spot. Have a good life."

CHAPTER 3

It was nearly one-thirty by the time they drove up to Jeremiah's house. Jeremiah thanked both his new friends for the adventure and ran to the door.

He burst into the kitchen. "Mom! How come you're home in the middle of the day?"

Jeremiah stopped. Nina's hair was a mess and her eyes were red. She was standing on a step stool putting dented cans of creamed corn in the cupboard. She got them cheaply from Mason's Supermarket, where she worked as a checker. The corn was okay, but the store couldn't sell dented cans.

"I have to work this evening. I took off a few hours before I go in," she answered softly.

"What's wrong?"

"Things." His mother took a deep breath and forced a smile. "You must have had a good time. Your face is dirty enough. Look at that mud on your pants. Hand me those cans, will you?"

"Wait until you hear this. We turned some animals loose at this place called the Sink. One of them was Spot. Mom, you wouldn't believe that place. It looks just like a Louisiana bayou, and it's right here in the middle of Indiana. It's just like the pictures I saw in a magazine Bill gave me."

Jeremiah handed her the damaged cans off the table. He could tell that she was very upset about something.

"Listen to this. This'll cheer you up. Charlie needs some pictures of the Sink for a report for the state. I told him you'd take them."

Nina stopped. "Jeremiah, I'm not good enough. You've got to be kidding."

Jeremiah was about to say, "Of course, you're good enough. We've taken pictures together all over the world." But he knew she wouldn't understand that part of his fantasy world.

"You're good enough, Mom. Charlie said he'd call you."

She patted Jeremiah's shoulder and said nothing.

◈ ◈ ◈

They ate lunch in silence. Jeremiah couldn't imagine why his mother was so disturbed. She had that faraway look that she had when she was disappointed in him. He couldn't think of anything he had done that would make her feel that way.

They did the dishes together then Nina said, "Jeremiah, your room is still a mess. And Bill wants you to come over as soon as I leave for work. Please go up and finish cleaning it before I leave."

As Jeremiah tried to find places for all the things Todd and he had left in his room, he played the events of the day over in his head. He wished he could phone Todd like he used to.

His mind kept returning to Charlie and Rita. *Why did Charlie think Rita was a radical? And what was that stuff about seven generations?*

He found the magazine with the bayou pictures in it. He became absorbed in the wonders of the photos. He heard his mother coming up the stairs.

"Jeremiah, we need to talk."

"Okay, Mom. What's up?"

She carried a large, rumpled manila envelope. "This came in the mail yesterday. I've been fretting about it ever since, but I just couldn't give it to you. I didn't want to spoil your time with Todd."

She handed him the package. It had come back—back from Eugene, Oregon; back from Tacoma, Washington; back from San Francisco. "Forwarding Order Expired" was stamped all over it. It was filled with letters he had written to his dad, letters that contained his innermost thoughts.

"What's in this, Jeremiah?"

"Nothing, Mom."

Tears were rolling down his mother's cheeks. He hoped she couldn't see his.

"I'm sorry, hon."

"It's okay."

"Oh, Jeremiah, I worry that I'm not taking good care of you. I know you need your father."

"I knew something was bothering you," Jeremiah said. "It's okay. I don't care about the divorce." But that was a lie.

His mother brushed her hand along his cheek and kissed his forehead. "I have to go to work now. Would you take out the trash before you go to Bill's?"

"Sure, Mom." His voice cracked. "You take good care of me, Mom. We take care of each other. We're a team, right?"

"You are such a sweetie," she said with a sigh. She gave him a big hug, spun and quickly left the room.

▩ ▩ ▩

The house was quiet and empty—emptier than he had ever known it. He went downstairs and started to collect the trash. He filled one bag and carried it to the curb. He went to his room and emptied the wastebasket into another bag. All the time he was in his room, the crumpled brown envelope on his bed mocked him.

He had tried so hard to keep in touch with his dad. He had sent silly little letters every other Sunday for two years. Those hadn't come back. Now, when he had sent the letters he really cared about, they came back. Packleruma!

He made another trip to the street. As he shoved the second bag into the overflowing trash can, a thought flashed through his mind. He whirled around and rushed back upstairs. He grabbed the brown envelope and ran back to the trash can. He stabbed the envelope into the trash bag with such force that a corner of it protruded through the plastic.

"There!" he said. "I'm not going to think about this anymore."

He said it, but it wasn't true. He was miserable. He thought about it all the way down the alley to Bill Loker's antique repair shop.

So what? he thought. *Mom and I are a team. I've got Todd, Bill, Charlie and Rita. What do I need a father for?*

Jeremiah came out of his daze as he approached the shop and realized that the shop's sign was missing. He stood for a moment with his hands on his hips and wondered. It had always been there.

The shop was his second home and Bill was the closest thing he had to a grandfather. As long as he could remember, as long as his mother could remember, Bill and Ruth were there for them.

He opened the door and went into the shop. Other times he would have stood against the tape measure Bill had put there so Jeremiah could see how much he had grown. This time he didn't.

"Hi, Bill," Jeremiah said softly.

Bill was painting. The brush looked tiny in his huge hand. He wiped his hands on a paint rag and stuck it into the back pocket of his bib overalls. He ran a hand through his salt and pepper hair.

"Come over here, J.S. I want to show you something."

Bill grabbed a corner of a plastic drop cloth that covered a large object resting on two sawhorses. He yanked it off, revealing the missing shop sign. Where it once had said "Loker's Antiques," it now had these freshly painted words:

LOKER & STOKELY ANTIQUES

"What do you think, J.S.?" Bill said. He put his hands on his hips and beamed proudly.

"What does it mean?"

"I always wanted the sign to say 'Wm. Loker and Son,' but Ruth and I never had any children. You're the closest we'll ever come to having a son."

Jeremiah stared at the sign. "I don't get it."

"I had a long talk with your mother. She thinks it would be a good idea if you had something to work for, especially this summer. I suggested that you learn the antique repair business."

"You didn't just do this so I won't think you're my babysitter, did you?"

"Heck no, J.S. I expect you to do your share of the work around here. I'm getting to the place in my life where I need some dependable help."

"I've always helped you anyway. You've always helped me, too. Isn't that good enough?"

"I thought you'd like the idea." Bill sounded disappointed.

"Well, I do like it. I just don't get it."

Jeremiah stared at the floor and wrote his initials in the saw-dust with his toe. He wondered if there was more to the proposal than Bill was telling him.

Bill wadded up the plastic drop cloth and pitched it to one side. "I know you have big plans for this summer," he said. "You have baseball, lawns to mow, and all those other things you do. But your mom and I thought that if you came here the first thing each day and worked in the shop for a couple of hours, the summer might go faster for you, and it would certainly help me out."

"Is this because Todd's gone and Mom thinks I'll get into trouble? Did she tell you about the letters?"

Bill looked squarely at Jeremiah's face. He didn't do that often. Most of the time, Bill talked while he was gluing a chair or sanding a piece of antique furniture.

"Okay, J.S., you've found us out. She did tell me that a package you sent to your dad came back." Bill motioned for Jeremiah to sit beside him on a low painting bench. "Your mother works very hard at Mason's. It's not easy doing it all alone. She's around a lot of other single mothers like herself. Some of their children have gotten into big trouble like drugs and fights. Even in a small town like East Newport, there are dangers that didn't used to exist. It would give her peace of mind if she knew you were here every morning."

"She could have just told me to come here. You didn't have to make me a partner. I didn't even know that a kid could be a partner in a real business."

"Of course, they can. Don't forget about your secret project. When you just hang out here, I don't pay you. But as a junior part-ner, well . . ."

Only two people knew his secret, Bill and Todd. After the di-vorce, his mother had to sell her camera to pay the rent. With it went her dream of becoming a professional photographer. He had prom-ised himself right then and there to get her a new, even better cam-era. So far, everything he tried had failed. One moneymaking scheme after another had come to a miserable end. Not the least of his problems was that a few weeks ago, when his financial situation was brighter, he had placed a camera in layaway and now it looked as if he would lose his deposit. If that happened, the only place his mom would ever be a professional photographer was in his daydreams.

"I'd have made you a partner some day anyway," Bill said. "It's a good idea to know woodworking. You'll be going off to college before you know it. But woodworking is always a useful skill, no matter what your life's work is."

Bill struggled to his feet. "What do you say, J.S.? Do we give this partnership a try? You don't need to tell your mother you saw through our scam."

"You'll teach me to use the power equipment?"

"Yes, I'll teach you to use the power equipment."

"You'll still tell me stories about my grandparents?"

"I'll still do that."

"You'll help me make a bunch of bluebird houses?"

"Bird houses?" Bill looked at Jeremiah quizzically. "How did that get into the conversation?"

"That's what I wanted to talk to you about. Do you know about the Sink?"

"Know about it? Your grandfather and I used to trap muskrats in Hog Creek. I've walked every square inch of that place."

"I went there yesterday with Charlie Willig and Rita Cuzak."

"You did? You met Bluebird?"

"We *saw* a bluebird."

"Rita's a Native American—Miami nation. Bluebird is her Indian name."

"Really? So that's what she meant. How do you know her?"

"I've known her all her life. Do you like her?"

"She's okay, I guess. Sure knows a lot about animals. Charlie called her a radical. What did he mean by that?"

Bill smiled. "The Miami nation isn't officially recognized as a tribe. She's very active in tribal politics to try to get that changed." Bill stood up and touched the newly painted sign to see if it was dry.

"She said something I didn't understand—something about seven generations," Jeremiah said.

"Many Indian tribes view nature that way. They always think seven generations ahead. They don't do anything that might cause hardship that far in the future. We ought to live that way ourselves. Help me get the sign off these sawhorses, will you?"

Jeremiah grabbed one end of the sign and Bill removed the sawhorses.

"Charlie wants to turn the Sink into a state park."

"I wish him luck. It should have been protected long before now."

From where Jeremiah stood, he could see the neat piles of wood in the scrap room. "He told me that if there were bird houses down there, bluebirds might make a comeback."

"Where are you thinking of putting them?"

"Near that old barn on the hill. Will you help me, then?"

They stood the sign on end just inside the door of the shop and Jeremiah stacked the sawhorses against the back wall.

"It's worth looking into. Just putting them there isn't enough, you know. You have to take care of them, keep them clean and repaired and all."

"It's such a cool place, though. We saw some deer and there's a beaver dam. I've never seen any place like it except in pictures of the bayou country."

"Do you know how to build a bird house?" Bill put his hands on his back. He stretched and groaned.

"I can get some books from the library."

"Sounds like a plan to me," Bill said.

"So we can do it?" Jeremiah said in an excited voice.

"Just be careful you don't disappear into the quicksand."

"Quicksand?"

"Just kidding, J.S. Used to hear talk about people going there and being gobbled up by the earth. There's an Indian legend about a whole tribe vanishing. "

"How could anyone think that?"

"Rita thinks there is some truth to the legend. And you've got to remember how the land looked a hundred and fifty years ago. The marsh was originally about twenty-seven miles long, about as wide, and dangerous."

"Twenty-seven miles? What happened to it? Did it sink?"

"No, it's mostly farm land now. You can still see it from the air, though."

"I thought we could use your scrap wood to make the houses," Jeremiah said. "That would be a good way for you to teach me to use the power equipment."

"Kill two birds with one stone, huh?" Bill said. He struck himself on the forehead with the heel of his hand. "Sorry, J.S. That just slipped out. You don't talk to a naturalist about killing birds. Bird houses made from scraps, huh? Good idea, kid. Very environmentally correct."

Naturalist! Jeremiah had never thought of himself that way. *Jeremiah Stokely, Naturalist. It has a nice ring to it.*

"I told Harvey Sidell I'd pick up some furniture at his house at three-thirty. Do you want to go along, or do you want to mind the shop?"

"I have to mow Mrs. Lennis' yard this afternoon."

"I doubt we'd be back until evening. You can stay and straighten up the scrap room if you want," Bill said. He hung his apron on a nail by the table saw and started to leave. Then he walked back. He had an old *National Geographic* magazine in his hand. "This is the last one of these things I'm going to get for you. If you're going to be in the antique business, you've got to learn to do your own wheeling and dealing."

Bill fumbled in the pocket of his worn bib overalls and came up with a key ring. "Here, partner. You'll need this. I must warn you, though. I put an alarm on all the power equipment. If you start a machine when I'm not here, it sends an automatic signal to the police station and they'll come and haul you off, screaming and kicking."

"Message received, Bill. Over and out."

"Just pull the door closed when you go. It'll lock. See you in the morning, partner?"

"See you in the morning."

◈ ◈ ◈

The shop had a hollow, eerie silence about it with Bill gone. Jeremiah had always put those two things together in his mind. The shop meant Bill and Bill meant the shop.

He sat down on the largest pile of boards and looked at the February, 1977, *National Geographic* Bill had just given him. The cover story was about the largest hot-air balloon anyone had ever tried to fly. He leafed through the magazine and stopped at a picture of an owl.

It was in an article that featured John Audubon's notebook. Jeremiah studied the strange writing in the picture. "He wrote both ways on the paper!" Jeremiah said to himself. "How neat! It's almost like a code."

Suddenly, he knew how he would use the blank book his mother had given him for his birthday: he'd keep a nature journal. He'd write about birds and plants just like John Audubon did. And he would start with the creatures he had seen in the Sink.

No, he'd start with a creature he *took* to the Sink—Spot.

CHAPTER FOUR

Jeremiah parked his bike at the shop just as Bill was turning over the "Yes, We're Open" sign. This time as he entered he did lean up against the tape measure.

"Have you grown another foot, J.S.?" Bill asked.

"Dumb joke, Bill. I *have* grown another head, though. Look where the mark was when I was nine," Jeremiah said with a voice full of pride.

"Don't suppose you're any smarter now." Bill pulled a handful of papers from the pocket of his bib overalls. "Look what I found— bluebird house plans."

"Great! Let me see them."

Bill spread the plans out on a workbench so they could study them.

Jeremiah took a tape measure to the scrap room to look for some likely pieces. Choosing an armload of boards, he hurried back to the bench. Bill cut several pieces of the various sizes shown on the plans and Jeremiah organized them. He put all the fronts in one pile, sides in another, bottoms and roof in their separate piles.

"Too bad you don't have your power tool safety book with you— the one I gave you for your birthday," Bill said.

"Ah, but I do. It's in the saddlebag on my bike," Jeremiah answered.

"In that case, it's time for you to learn to use the drill press."

Armed with the book and a little additional instruction from Bill, Jeremiah drilled the inch-and-a-half hole in all nine front pieces.

The actual assembly didn't take long and before it was time for him to leave to go to his ball game, they had nine finished bird houses lined up on the floor.

"J. S., I call that mass production. Henry Ford would be proud."

Bill was still admiring their handiwork when Jeremiah left to go to his game.

◫ ◫ ◫

Hampton Park's baseball complex consisted of four diamonds. Jeremiah's games were always played on diamond "C," right next to the girls' softball diamond. Stacy's team was in the field. He still had ten minutes before his own game, so he sat on the bleachers to watch a little of hers. He always wondered why boys played baseball and girls played softball. Stacy was a good athlete, better than most of the boys on his team. They had played tee-ball together. But now she played softball and he played baseball.

Stacy played third base. Her team wore blue and white striped uniforms with short pants. The long blue socks stopped at the knee—just below the adhesive bandage on Stacy's leg. Her auburn hair sneaked out from the back of her cap and swayed rhythmically as she moved from side to side, concentrating on the game.

The bat cracked. The ball soared toward the outfield. Stacy took three steps backward, caught the ball and rifled it to second, catching the runner off base.

"Double play!" Jeremiah said. He jumped up and shouted, "Awright, Stacy!"

Stacy glanced his way for just an instant, then she turned her attention back to the game. Jeremiah knew how she felt. It was good to hear a familiar voice in the crowd.

Jeremiah's teammates were gathering. He helped carry the equipment into the dugout.

"Hey, Stokely," Brad said. "You've got Todd's mitt. How come?"

"He gave it to me." Jeremiah removed the mitt from his bike and fastened it to the belt loop of his gray-striped uniform.

"Well, it's sure better than that raggy old thing you've been using."

"My mitt is okay. I've caught a lot of your fly balls with it."

"What a crock. You probably got it at a yard sale."

"Shut up, Brad," Jeremiah said softly. His mitt was a touchy subject. His mother had bought it for him, and he knew it was a cheap imitation of the real thing. His mother didn't know it. She didn't know that having an inferior mitt was worse than not having one at all. But he wore it proudly, simply because not doing so would have hurt his mother's feelings.

❖ ❖ ❖

It wasn't a very good game. Jeremiah's team, the Mason Red Sox, led five to nothing by the fourth inning. The only excitement came in the fifth inning. Jeremiah walked, then Brad came to bat. On Brad's second strike, Jeremiah stole second base. The catcher tried to make the throw to second, but instead threw the ball into center field. Jeremiah sped around second and was safe at third.

On the next pitch, Brad doubled and Jeremiah made it home easily. As he crossed the plate, he heard Stacy cheering from the bleachers.

Jeremiah's run was the final one. The game ended with a six-nothing win. He and Brad congratulated each other.

Stacy rode up to them on her bike. "What happened to your eye, Jeremiah?"

"He got smart with me and I punched him out, Red," Brad said.

"Don't call me Red," Stacy protested.

"He didn't either, Stacy. I hit myself with a door."

"Sure you did, Stokely. I'll see you guys. Coach is taking me home."

Jeremiah strapped Todd's mitt to his handlebars.

"I saw you in that state truck the other day. What were you doing? " Stacy asked. She pulled her bike alongside Jeremiah's.

"Stacy, I found the coolest place in the whole world. It's not far from your grandmother's house. Want to go there?"

"I promised Gramby I'd come home for lunch right after the game. What is this place anyway?"

"A swamp."

"You think a swamp is cool?" Stacy pretended to be in deep thought. "Yeah, I guess you *would* think swamps are cool."

"It is, though, Stacy. It looks like Louisiana. We could ride our bikes down the old railroad bed. You can see most of it from there."

"Ride our bikes down a railroad? Are you nuts?"

"The tracks have been taken up. It's just like riding on a hill."

"I'll ask Gramby. Maybe we could take sandwiches and pop."

"Let's do it," he said. He jumped on his bike. "I'll race you to the beauty shop."

He popped a wheelie and raced to the road. Stacy cut across the grass and caught up to him by the time he turned out of the park and headed down Elm. They struggled side by side until Jeremiah saw they weren't going to make the green light at Wysor. He swerved into the alley and raced across Mason's parking lot. He ended up half a block ahead of her by the time the light changed. He was sitting on the curb in front of her grandmother's business when Stacy rode up.

They were both out of breath.

Stacy plopped down beside him on the grass. "I have just one thing to say to you, Jeremiah Stokely."

"What's that?"

"You cheat!"

Stacy's Grandmother Hunter was washing a customer's hair when they entered the shop.

"How was the game, Stacy?" her grandmother asked. In some ways, Mrs. Hunter reminded Jeremiah of Bill. She talked as she worked and she looked about Bill's age. She used a lot of the same expressions, too. Her speech had what Bill called a Hoosier twang.

"We lost, but Jeremiah's team won," Stacy said. She sat down in a hair dryer chair.

"Congratulations, Jeremiah," Mrs. Hunter said. She turned off the rinse spray and sat the customer upright in the chair.

"Gramby, Jeremiah and I want to take a bike ride. Can I fix some sandwiches?"

"You have a piano lesson this afternoon, young lady."

"I know. We won't go far."

"Make sure you don't," Mrs. Hunter said. Then she turned to

the customer and said, "I swear, if I didn't tell that child to stay close to home, she would ride her bike to Chicago. How's your mother, Jeremiah? She hasn't been in for a long time."

"She's fine, ma'am." Jeremiah didn't want to tell Stacy's grand-mother that Ruth Loker worked on his mother's hair. When there isn't much money, groceries—even dented cans, broken boxes, and day-old bread—come before beauty parlors.

In the kitchen, Stacy threw together two cold-cut sandwiches. She took two cans of pop from the refrigerator, and out the back door they went.

The two pushed their bikes while they wolfed down the sand-wiches, then took off in the direction of the Sink.

It was easier riding down the old railroad bed than Jeremiah had expected. Recent tire tracks made a natural bike path for them.

"This is like a trail in a park, Jeremiah."

"My friend Charlie wants to make it into a state park."

The shrubs along the side of the rail bed became denser. As they approached Hog Creek, Jeremiah saw the same car he had seen there the other day. They leaned their bikes against the iron trestle of the bridge.

"Gramby gave me a book called *Girl of the Limberlost*. It's about a swamp. She read it when she was my age."

Jeremiah stood at the edge of the embankment. "Bill and I are making bluebird houses to put here."

Stacy moved cautiously to the edge of the steep slope. "Can we get down there?"

"Sure. Come on." Jeremiah leaped over the edge of the railway bed. The first few feet were covered with large stones where the ties used to rest. After that, wild plants took over.

Stacy followed him down the ridge to the edge of the creek. They stopped at the foot of the large sycamore tree that slanted over the water.

Jeremiah grabbed a low-hanging branch and swung himself into the tree. Stacy was right behind him. They held their arms out straight, like Olympic gymnasts on a balance beam, and walked to the place where a branch curved upward. They sat and dangled their feet over the water. From this vantage point, they could see the fascinating world of the Sink.

"That's the hill where we saw the bluebird yesterday," Jeremiah said. He pointed to the south of the hill. "You can see the end of the beaver dam."

"What's that you said about bird houses?"

"I'm building a bunch of them from the scrap wood in Bill's shop. Charlie says they will attract bluebirds. I'm bringing the first load down here tomorrow."

"I'll help. Shelly and I go to church with Gramby. After that I don't have anything to do." Stacy pulled herself into a fork between two large branches and leaned back as nicely as if she were in a lawn chair.

"Will your grandmother let you?"

"Gramby lets me do more than Dad does—even more than Mama does."

"I wish I had grandparents. Mom's parents were killed in a car wreck before I was born. I don't know anything about my dad's parents."

"Let me tell you about grandparents. I have eight of them."

"Eight? Get outa here!"

"No, I really do. Gramby and Gramp are Dad's parents. Mama is really my stepmother. Her mom and dad live in Indianapolis. Shelly and I go there every summer for two weeks. I call my real mom Julie and my stepfather Harold. All their parents live in Chicago. When Julie's aunt died, everybody came to our house and I had eight grandparents in one room at the same time."

"I didn't know your parents were divorced. I thought I was the only kid with that problem."

"It's not much of a problem anymore. I don't really remember when Julie lived with us. I was just two when she left."

"How come she left?"

"I guess she wanted to go to Chicago and Dad didn't. I don't like to visit her. She lives in a seventh floor apartment. There aren't even supposed to be kids in the building. There's no yard and no place to ride a bike."

"I'd give anything to visit my dad. I don't even know where he is." Jeremiah yanked a leaf from the sycamore tree and started pulling the points off it. The image of the brown envelope sticking out of the trash bag flitted through his mind.

Suddenly Stacy whispered, "Look!" She pointed to the water ten feet below where they sat. A mother duck swam through the reeds at the edge of Hog Creek, chattering to three ducklings that followed her in single file as if tied together on a string.

They were so intent on the family of ducks that they failed to see the two men come out of the bushes and stand at the bottom of the sycamore tree.

"Hey, what are you kids doing here? Who are you?"

Jeremiah turned so quickly that he nearly lost his balance on the limb. Before he could say anything, a large man who looked like a linebacker for the Indianapolis Colts said, "You get yourselves down here right now!"

The other man carried surveyor's instruments. He wore a yellow hard hat and was shaking a can of spray paint. He was much smaller than the linebacker and had a thin mustache.

Stacy slid down the tree. Jeremiah hung from the branch and dropped to the ground.

"I know you. You're the boy who was here with that state guy, aren't you?" Linebacker said.

"Yes, day before yesterday."

"I don't want you kids hanging around here. We're going to be moving some heavy equipment in and you'd better not mess with it." He stepped away from the sycamore tree and Hard Hat sprayed a vibrant orange "X" on its trunk.

Jeremiah's heart sank. "How come you're painting this tree?" he asked.

"We're going to cut it down so we can move the equipment in, of course," Linebacker said.

"But my friend said they were going to make this a park," Jeremiah protested.

"I wish that guy would get off that idea. This place ain't good for nothing. It just breeds mosquitoes and snakes."

"We're leaving now, but we'll be back. I don't want to see your faces around here again. You got it? C'mon, Harry." Linebacker pushed his way through the brush, followed by Harry, who was still shaking the spray can.

"I can't believe they're going to cut down our tree," Stacy said.

"Charlie isn't going to believe it either." Jeremiah threw a twig into Hog Creek. Suddenly he said, "Stacy! What time is your lesson?"

"Oh, no, I forgot all about it. Gramby will kill me if I'm late. I've got a recital a week from tomorrow."

They scrambled up the embankment to their bikes.

"How come we came down out of our tree just because that man told us to? We don't even know those guys," Jeremiah said.

"We're kids. Kids have to do what everybody tells them," she said as she sped down the path.

Jeremiah took one last look at the Sink. To his astonishment, he saw dozens of trees with orange "Xs" painted on them. "Packleruma!" he said.

⊡ ⊡ ⊡

It was slow going on the trail back to the street. The wind had picked up and they were riding directly into it.

Once they turned onto the gravel road, they said no more and pedaled hard away from the Sink. They skidded down the gravel road and battled the headwind up Broadway. At last, they struggled up the hill to the beauty shop.

Stacy's piano teacher was just getting out of his car as they arrived.

"Whew," Stacy sighed. She leaned her bicycle against the porch. "I'll call you about tomorrow."

Jeremiah gave her thumbs-up and rode home. He was upset about the trees being taken out of the Sink, especially since he had just discovered it. *Why would anyone want to mess up such a great place?*

He tried to call Charlie as soon as he got home to tell him about the men marking the trees for cutting. He got the answering machine, so he left a message for Charlie to call him. He grabbed a banana and went to the back porch.

He looked across the vacant lot. The wind he and Stacy had

pedaled against had brought with it huge dark clouds, and the sun made golden halos around them. The filtered light made a peculiar glow around the horse chestnut tree in the vacant lot next door. He couldn't resist walking through the high grass to his favorite spot under the tree.

This was his hideaway, his place to think, his place to dream. He had been going there since he was little and could not imagine that he would ever stop. He had launched some of his best fantasies under this tree.

He gazed across the vacant lot. So peaceful! The tall grass swayed in the wind and the swirling clouds calmed his mind. He forgot about the men who were going to cut the trees in the Sink. He forgot about not knowing where his dad was. He just leaned back against the tree and closed his eyes.

How long he sat there, he didn't know. Time was different for him under the horse chestnut tree. Now the wind grew cooler. Lightning crashed in the west and he ran for the safety of home.

The phone was ringing as he entered the kitchen. It was his mother.

"I'm at the college library picking up some books about nature photography. I might be kind of late. I called earlier. Were you gone?"

"I just went to the horse chestnut tree. I thought it was going to rain, so I came home."

"Thinking great thoughts or dreaming great dreams?"

"Probably neither," he said in a small voice.

"I'm still sad about the letters, too. Here's a hug for you. See you in a few."

"See you."

There was nothing on TV, so he grabbed a box of raisins and took them to his room. He pulled the blank book from the shelf, opened it to the first page and printed in large letters, "Notes and Sketches by Jeremiah Stokely, Naturalist." Then at the bottom of the page he wrote, "Just like the notes of John J. Audubon."

He put on the headset of Todd's CD player and thought about his adventures at the Sink. He remembered the Audubon article, and began to write:

My friends and I drove to the place where the ground sinks into itself. We were there to set free some animals that Rita made well.

One of them was an owl I saved. I called her Spot.

It was hard to set Spot free, but I knew it was time to do it. It made Rita sad to turn her animals loose, too. There is a chance that her fox will kill her rabbits. But she told me that's the way nature works.

Bill told me once that a cowboy never named his horse because he might have to eat it. It's hard to hurt something or someone if you know them well enough to call them by name.

Stacy said something like that, too. She is afraid they are going to cut down our tree. Before she called it OUR tree, it was just a tree. Now it's a special tree.

It's easy to climb and has great places to sit. A family of ducks swam right under our feet.

He read what he had written. Then he turned the book sideways and started writing in the other direction.

I guess I like nature so much because of all the stories Bill tells me about Henry David Somebody. Henry liked nature, too. He said wilderness is the promise of the future. Bill has told me this lots of times. I think Charlie believes it, too. That is why he wants to turn the Sink into a wild place for plants and animals.

I'm going to help Charlie. Bill and I made nine bird houses using scraps. It's a good idea to use scrap so no trees have to be cut down to make the houses.

Mom is going to take pictures for Charlie's report about the Sink. Stacy wants to help, too.

He heard his mother come in, put her tote bag on the table and open the silverware drawer.

"Jeremiah, I brought ice cream," she called. "Are you interested?"

He closed his journal. Three quick steps brought him to the stairs. With hands on both railings, he slid all the way down.

"That was quick," Nina said. She dipped the ice cream for him and for herself. She sagged onto a chair, pulled off her shoes and rested her feet on the rungs of Jeremiah's chair.

"I'm so tired," she gasped. "I've got to get a different job."

"Like what, Mom?"

"Like anything."

"Like a nature photographer?"

"I wish."

CHAPTER FIVE

Jeremiah heard his mother moving around in the kitchen. It was her turn to prepare Sunday breakfast. He thought about how their little breakfast game got started. He was in the third grade and had chicken pox. His mother had fixed a tray with cereal, orange juice, milk and a couple of graham crackers for later. He was so sick that he really didn't enjoy it, but he pretended he did.

The following Sunday, he got up early and prepared the same meal for her. Since then, they had taken turns every week. In that time, they had missed only one Sunday when Jeremiah stayed at Bill and Ruth's. His dad had come back to town to pick up the rest of his things. It was before Bill finished remodeling the big stone house where they lived. Jeremiah spent that entire weekend sitting on a scaffold between two ladders looking out the bay window, watching for his dad. He never showed up.

The other part of the Sunday ritual, writing to his dad, had come later. It was only after Jeremiah realized that his dad wasn't coming home that this became a part of every Sunday's activities. Now there was no point in writing letters that couldn't be delivered. He knew it. His mother knew it. He thought about what he would say if his mother mentioned it. *If she says anything, I'm going to tell her that I'm not going to do it. I'll write to Todd, but I'm not writing Dad!*

"Jeremiah," his mother called from the foot of the stairs. "Are you ready for this wondermous Louisiana breakfast?"

"Louisiana breakfast?" Jeremiah asked.

She stopped just inside the door and placed the tray on Todd's junk box. She put her hands on her hips, looked at the box, looked at Jeremiah, then again at the box.

"Okay, Mom. I'll put the stuff away. What's for breakfast?"

"Since you seem to have such a fascination for the bayou country, we're going to have ourselves a Louisiana bayou phantasmagoria! I picked up this used CD at the college bookstore." She pressed the eject button on the boom box and stuck in a disk. She turned on the music, the kind of Delta blues that she liked so much, then brought the tray to him. "We have scrambled eggs with some original Cajun Tabasco sauce, hush puppies, tomato juice, milk, mood music, and best of all—grits."

"Grits? What are grits?"

"Grits are groceries." She pretended to hold a microphone to her lips and sang in a bluesy voice, "If I don't love you, baby, eggs ain't poultry, grits ain't groceries, and Mona Lisa was a man."

"Funny, Mom. Very funny. What's grits?"

"It's a southern dish made from ground-up parched corn. I know we don't eat them often—well, never—but grits are good for you. And we had a broken shipment, so I got the box for nothing."

Jeremiah stirred the pile of white lumpy stuff with his fork.

"Why is it called 'grits' like it's lots of things? It looks like one big blob to me. Can you get just one grit?"

"Now who's being funny? Try the grits. You just might like them." She went back down to the kitchen and returned with another tray and sat on the foot of his bed. The strange music filled the room.

"You're pretty, Mom."

"Well, thank you, Jeremiah. You're not bad looking yourself." She kissed the tips of her fingers and blew the kiss to him. "Whatever possessed you to say that?"

"I don't know." He did know, though. He had overheard Ruth tell her once, "Nina, you're a very pretty woman. Why don't you find a young man and go out on a date now and then? You know you can leave Jeremiah here." His mother had just laughed.

"Well, thank you for the compliment, anyway."

His mother seemed to be lost in the music that filled the room. He had never heard anything like it before. He watched her as she measured the rhythm with her fork between bites.

"Do you have plans for today, Jeremiah?"

"We have nine bluebird houses done. I'm going to take them to the Sink."

"Are you sure it's okay for you to be doing that?"

"Sure. Charlie said it was a good idea. He'll help me put them up where they belong. He told me just to fill up the boat."

"You be very careful, kiddo. Especially around boats. Here, let me get your tray. Did you like the grits?"

Jeremiah grinned. "Can I take the Fifth Amendment?"

Nina smiled and took the trays to the kitchen.

The phone rang.

"Jeremiah, it's for you, hon."

Jeremiah tripped over the end of the sheet as he got out of bed. He ran down the stairs, two steps at a time.

"It's a *girl*," Nina whispered.

Jeremiah made a face at her.

"Jeremiah?" Stacy said.

"Hi, Stacy, what's up?"

"Are you going to take the bird houses to the Sink today?"

"Yep. I'm going to Bill's in a while to pick them up."

His mother stood at the sink rinsing dishes. She looked at him sideways. "Not until you take a bath, you aren't," she whispered.

"Gramby said I could help after church," Stacy said.

"Meet me at Bill Loker's shop. I'll have them ready to go by then."

Jeremiah hung up, slammed his cap on his head and turned the bill around backwards. His blond hair squirted out over his forehead.

"Just where do you think you're going?" his mother said.

He took off the cap. "It was worth a try."

"Not even close, partner. Take a bath and don't forget—clean underwear!"

"Oh, Mom! I know," he grunted in disgust.

⊡ ⊡ ⊡

Jeremiah raked a comb through his damp hair. Before he left, he rummaged through the junk drawer in the kitchen for some twine to tie the houses to his bike. His mother was reading the Sunday paper.

"Garfield's good today. Be careful down there," she said. "I just remembered that Bill and Ruth are gone. How are you going to get the houses?"

"You forget that I'm Bill's junior partner," he said, dangling a key ring in front of her face.

"Don't stay away too long, Jeremiah. I'll order pizza," she said. She grabbed his hand and pulled him close for a hug. "Don't get in any trouble."

"Oh, Mom. I know what I'm doing."

He ran out the back door and counted his steps to see how far he could get down the walk before he heard the slam. He took fourteen steps, all the way to his bike, and still the door had not closed.

He went back to the porch to find out why. "Broken spring," he said. "I'll have to fix that." He closed and latched the door.

⊡ ⊡ ⊡

He had the bird houses stacked up on the sidewalk outside the antique shop by the time Stacy arrived. He realized that they were going to be a bigger load than he expected. He eyed the houses and the carrier on the back of his bike.

"You really think we can carry all those houses?" Stacy asked.

"It'll be close. I brought string to tie them on. I'll make them fit."

Stacy held her bike as Jeremiah made twine slings so the houses could swing below her handlebars. She leaned her bike against the shop and steadied Jeremiah's bike while he tied on the remaining bird houses.

The load was cumbersome and Jeremiah wobbled, but finally he got the load under control and pedaled down the alley.

They got up a little speed on Madison Street, but the force of a strong wind on Broadway slowed them down. It took all their riding skill to keep their balance.

They struggled past Gramby's beauty shop and turned onto Jackson, riding toward the Sink.

The turn onto Jackson made Stacy's houses swing against her front wheel. She braked and steered to the right. Jeremiah was following too closely and his front wheel rubbed Stacy's back wheel. They lost control on a patch of loose gravel, slid sideways and came to rest in a pile of bird houses, upturned bicycle wheels and legs.

They lay there, helpless, laughing hysterically.

"Are you okay?" Jeremiah gasped.

"No." Stacy groaned and rubbed her knee. "Call me an ambulance."

"Okay, you're an ambulance," Jeremiah said, and the laughter started again.

Jeremiah was still flat on his back when a red Jeep Cherokee pulled up. The driver got out. It was Joseph Fowler. "Are you guys okay?"

Joseph helped Stacy up and lifted her bike off Jeremiah's chest. "What are you doing anyway, Jeremiah?"

"We're *trying* to take these bird houses to the Sink." Jeremiah lifted his bike and all the houses slid to the pavement.

"Who's your friend?"

"This is Stacy."

"Hi, Stacy. I'm . . ."

"I know who you are," Stacy said. "Everyone knows you."

"Put your stuff in the Jeep. I'll take you where you're going," Joseph offered.

They loaded the houses inside and Joseph strapped the bikes to the carrier on top. Jeremiah dusted himself off.

"I didn't know you knew Joseph Fowler, Jeremiah. Too cool!" Stacy whispered.

"Now, where you taking this stuff?" Joseph asked.

Jeremiah pointed the direction and they started east on Jackson. Stacy sat in the middle, beaming.

"The Sink is a swamp. It looks just like a bayou. My friend

Charlie Willig wants to turn it into a state park. We're helping by putting bluebird houses there."

They continued down the abandoned railway bed, deeper and deeper into the undergrowth.

"It's a wild place, all right," Joseph said. He stopped at the parking spot by the steel bridge and unloaded their bikes. He shielded his eyes from the afternoon sun and looked out over the Sink. Its shallow lake shimmered in the haze.

"You're right. It does look like a bayou," he said and handed the houses out to Stacy and Jeremiah. "Can you get back to town all right?" he asked.

Stacy lifted a bird house in each hand and moved them to the edge of the embankment. "No problem," she said. "We've been here on our bikes before. Thanks for the ride."

Joseph rolled down the window to wave goodbye. "If you have a load like that again, don't try to bring them on your bikes. Let me know. Okay?"

"Okay, we will," Jeremiah said and waved.

"Can you believe it? We actually rode out here with Joseph Fowler, the most popular boy in town!" Stacy said.

"I know! He lives across the street from me."

"You're kidding!"

Stacy waved once more and they scrambled down the embankment with a load of houses. It took two sweaty trips to carry all the houses through the tangle of weeds to Charlie's boat. Charlie would be by in the next couple days to put the houses up.

The two started back up the path toward their bikes. Jeremiah wiped his face on the tail of his T-shirt. Beads of perspiration glistened on Stacy's upper lip. When they came to their sycamore, they walked up its trunk and took their places on their favorite limbs, high above Hog Creek.

"Jeremiah, look!" Stacy stared off into the distance.

Jeremiah cupped his hands above his eyes and looked down Hog Creek where she pointed. He counted more than twenty trees sprayed with orange paint. There were an equal number of doomed trees on the opposite side of the stream.

"I know, Stacy. They want to cut down the whole place! Charlie will put a stop to it, though."

"What if he can't? What if he waits too long and they cut the trees down before the state takes over? What good is a state park without trees?"

Stacy put her hand on Jeremiah's arm. "When you told me about the Sink, I couldn't imagine why you were so excited. I mean, all I could think of was bugs and snakes, but now I know why you like it so much. It's beautiful. Where will we sit if they cut down *our* tree? Where will all the animals live?"

"They're not going to cut down the trees, Stacy. I promise you that."

They sat there for nearly an hour, basking in the beauty of the place. The sound of geese overhead and the green scent of nature surrounded them. Reluctantly, they came down from their perch and rode silently back to town.

CHAPTER SIX

There was a knock at the front door. His mother was on her knees, scrubbing the kitchen floor. She pushed a lock of hair from her sweaty forehead. "That's the pizza, Jeremiah. There's money on the counter. Pay him, will you?"

Jeremiah paid the delivery woman and brought the pizza in. His mother got a two-liter bottle of cola out of the refrigerator and two tumblers from the cabinet and pulled up a chair beside him. "Charlie just called, Jeremiah. He wants to come over this evening to talk about my taking the Sink pictures. You'll help me get the house straightened up, won't you?"

"The house is okay." He opened the pizza box. "Awright! Double cheese!"

"The house is *not* okay. I'm so far behind on my housework. "

Jeremiah pulled a wedge of pizza from the box and sank his teeth into it.

"You will help, won't you?"

"What do I have to do?"

"Stop talking with your mouth full, for starters. Run the sweeper in the living room and dust everything, okay? I'll take care of the kitchen and the bath. Don't even think about inviting him to your room."

"Cool, Mom," he said. He noticed the broken box of grits still on the counter top. They had grits for breakfast because it was free. They always had second-day bread and dented cans. But the pizza they were having for lunch cost nine dollars and eighty cents. They could have had several meals with that amount of money. *Why would Mom order such an expensive meal on Sunday? It doesn't make sense.*

He watched his mother bite the pointed end of her pizza and his question was answered. Her eyes closed, almost reverently. Jeremiah knew that while she was at work during the week, she rushed to the back room to catch a snack. Now that she was taking photography classes, she hardly ever sat down for a real meal. *She always leaves meals for me. This is the only time she thinks about herself. No wonder she wanted to spurge a little.*

❖ ❖ ❖

Jeremiah was just winding the cord onto the sweeper when he heard Charlie's car stop in front.

"He's here, Mom."

"Nuts! Already?" she said. She threw a dishtowel over the dishes in the drainer, wiped her hands on her jeans and ran for the bathroom. "Keep him occupied until I can get myself together, hon."

Jeremiah opened the door. Charlie carried a small box and a large roll of papers under his arm.

"Come on in, Charlie. Mom will be right out."

He handed Jeremiah the brown cardboard box. "Rita sent you a present."

"What is it?"

"Why do people always say that? Open it and find out."

Jeremiah folded back the lid and lifted out an earth-colored clay pot decorated with a row of owls around the top.

"Rita made that especially for you. She's a fine potter."

"Awesome! I know just where to put it. "He held it to the light and looked at it more closely. Rita had scratched in the bottom, "For Jeremiah, friend of owls." It was sighed, "Kiseleehsia."

"What does this mean?" Jeremiah asked. He showed the signature to Charlie.

"That's Rita's Indian name. It means Bluebird."

Jeremiah set the pot gently on the TV. "You'd better sit down, Charlie. I've got some really bad news."

"What's that, Jeremiah?"

"I took a bunch of bird houses to the Sink, and I saw that they're going to cut down every single tree along the creek."

"What?"

"There's an orange 'X' on lots of them. I know that means they're going to cut them down. Some men were out there painting them, and they chased Stacy and me away."

"Someone chased you away? Who was it?"

"I don't know. One of them looked like a linebacker. The other one's name was Harry."

"Mel Franklin and Harry Sloan, I bet—Franklin Tree Service. That *is* bad news."

"What's bad news?" Nina said as she entered the room. She was wearing a white shirt with silver buttons in the front, and a khaki skirt. Her dark hair was pulled back into a twist. She even wore lipstick.

Jeremiah stared. He hardly ever saw his mother in anything but her yellow Mason's checkout smock, or the scruffy clothes she wore to clean house, or the jeans she wore to class. He couldn't remember the last time he had seen her so dressed up.

"You look nice, Nina. Jeremiah was just telling me about the trees being marked for cutting in the Sink. That means we really do have to get down to business and get those pictures taken."

"They're going to cut down all the trees along the creek, Mom."

"What on earth for?" Nina asked.

"Some people won't be satisfied until every wild place in the world is paved," Charlie said.

"What now?" Nina said.

Charlie unrolled his papers on the living room floor. One was a large map of the Sink. It showed all the things that Jeremiah knew: the railroad bed, Hog Creek, the island hill and the shallow lake.

"This is what the Sink looks like now," Charlie said. "Now look at this."

He unrolled another map that was drawn on very thin paper and placed it over the first one. They could still see the features of the first map through the second.

"With this overlay map, you see here how the old railroad be-comes a bike trail. It connects with another trail over here that goes all the way to the Ohio River," Charlie said. "This is a trail along Hog Creek that leads to the boat landing. The ranger station goes there. The nature center, with a bird-watching room, will be on the hill. We'll control the water flow so it's always an island. You'll only be able to get there by boat. That's all the improvements we'll make. Everything else goes back to nature."

Jeremiah studied Charlie. Up to now he had only seen him in uniform. It occurred to him that seeing Charlie in an Arnold Palmer golf shirt was really seeing him for the first time.

Charlie's keen blue eyes brightened as he pointed out each highlight of the plan. A lock of curly brown hair jiggled over his forehead. "We really need the pictures, Nina. How soon can you take them?"

"I get off work at five tomorrow. I could go check out a camera and be ready by five-thirty. They say you get the best nature shots in the early morning or evening anyway."

"Okay. I'll pick you guys up and we'll do it," Charlie said.

"I can't go," Jeremiah said.

"Why not, hon?"

"I have a game at five-thirty."

Charlie stood, but left the plans spread out on the floor. "Okay, how does this sound? Your mom and I will go take the pictures and pick you up after the game and then we'll all go out someplace nice to eat."

Jeremiah could almost count on one hand the times he had eaten in a nice restaurant, and almost all of them were with Todd and Mr. Miller after a Reds game. He should have been excited. He and his mother never ate out. But somehow he wasn't pleased with Charlie's offer.

"You don't have to take us out. Besides, you don't even know if I can take good pictures," Nina said.

"Jeremiah recommends you highly."

"He's prejudiced. Would you like to see some of my work?"

Charlie nodded. Nina led him to the kitchen table where she had arranged the photos she thought he might like to see.

Jeremiah studied the plans again. The idea of a permanent island fascinated him. There was something mysterious about islands, especially islands where there were animals and strange plants.

He could pinpoint the spot on the map where the sycamore spread out over Hog Creek. He remembered what Stacy had said: *Where will we sit if they cut down our tree?* It *was* their tree. Not that they owned it. A person couldn't really own a tree. Yet, calling it "our tree" made a difference, the way Rita felt about "her" rabbits.

Jeremiah heard his mother explaining her photos to Charlie. She talked about composition, light quality, depth of field and angles of approach. It made Jeremiah feel warm inside to hear his mother so enthusiastic about something—anything. Yet, it hurt him that she was going to have to do this important work with a borrowed camera. That was his fault, and that bothered him a lot. Then, too, there was Charlie—this new Charlie he didn't know—listening to his mother's every word and smiling softly at her excitement.

It was eight-thirty when Charlie said, "Well, it's set then. I'll pick you up after work, and we'll shoot the pictures. Then we'll get Jeremiah and go eat at the Hermitage."

"Oh, but, Charlie," Nina protested. "The Hermitage is so expensive."

"Not to worry. It's my treat. It's the least I can do. After all, Jeremiah is my watchdog and you're going to take the pictures that will sell my bosses on the idea of a wetland park. And, let me remind you, I didn't offer to pay you for the pictures, so I owe you."

"That's good," Nina said with a smile. "This way I won't mess up my amateur status."

After Charlie left, Nina returned to her photos. Jeremiah finally got around to reading the Sunday comics. His eyes kept drifting to his mother, who hummed an old tune and looked strangely happy.

Jeremiah muted the TV and did a lot of channel surfing. He stopped to watch Tiger Woods birdie the ninth hole in some golf tournament. He turned to PBS, but reception was too poor. A message scrolled across the bottom of the screen: "The National Weather Service has issued a severe storm warning for the following . . ." Jeremiah turned off the TV.

He picked up the owl pot. "Mom, maybe we should get cable," he said.

"All right, dear."

She wasn't listening. If she had been, she would have said, "If we had the money . . ." She said that a lot.

He wondered what Todd was doing. Was he out in his canoe on Pigeon River? Maybe he was flipping channels, too, or playing Nintendo.

"Mom, I'm going upstairs."

"Okay, sweetie. I'll make popcorn after a while."

He reached for the boom box to start the music. He couldn't quite reach it, and in shifting position on the bed, he knocked over a stack of *National Geographic*s. They slid across the floor like a giant deck of cards, and stopped in a pile against Todd's junk box.

"Packleruma!" he said.

He remembered his mother's insistence that he do something about the junk box. *As Bill says, 'There's no time like the present.'*

He shoved the magazines back into an uneven stack, then he opened Todd's box and dragged the contents out onto his bed. Most of the things were easy to find a place for. He sorted the baseball cards and put them with his collection in the big blue notebook. He jammed the clippings and pictures into a drawer of his dresser. The rollerblades, pads and helmet went into the closet.

Small things found new homes. He had trouble finding a space large enough for the Junior Detective set. He finally decided that the fingerprint kit could go into a drawer, the detective booklet onto the shelf beside his nature journal, and the handcuffs could stay on the doorknob.

The room was stuffy and all this work made him hot. He opened the window for some fresh air and looked out past the horse chestnut tree. Dark storm clouds filtered the sunlight into long beams against the darkening sky. He saw the landing lights of a Cessna 170 banking to make its final approach to the small airfield south of his house. The engine revved and the small plane disappeared behind the trees and into his fantasy.

"Here's our plane, Mom," Jeremiah said. They stood on the tarmac as threatening clouds rolled in around them.

"Are you sure it will be okay? The weather service is predicting vio-

lent storms," Nina said.

"It'll be risky, but it's too good an opportunity to miss. Imagine, Mom, you are the official photographer for the world's largest blues festival in Lafayette, Louisiana."

The small plane rolled up in front of them. The pilot opened the door and shouted, "Get that stuff in here, folks. We've got to beat this storm."

Jeremiah handed him the photographic gear, and they boarded and bounced down the runway. The wind increased after they became airborne. The only light was the eerie glow of the instrument panel. The struggling engine whined in their ears. They were buffeted about in the small cabin. Jeremiah struggled to keep their gear from being thrown into the pilot's lap.

"It's getting too rough, folks. I've got to get above this bank of storm clouds," the pilot warned.

There was a loud snap. The engine stopped. The instrument panel went dark. They started slowly spinning toward the earth.

"I think we blew a fuse, Jeremiah," Nina said.

"All this stuff going on and you think it's just a fuse?"

"All what going on, Jeremiah?"

"Huh?"

The storm subsided and left only the darkness in his room. His mother stood at the top of the stairs holding a flashlight. "I was going to make popcorn, but I think I blew a fuse. Would you go down to the basement and see if you can fix it?"

CHAPTER SEVEN

Bill called and told Jeremiah it was an important day and they needed to get an early start. He ate a quick breakfast—no grits. His mother was still in the bathroom getting ready for work.

Jeremiah yelled, "Going to the shop, Mom. See you after the game." His bike had a flat tire and he didn't have time to fix it, so Jeremiah had to walk to the shop.

Bill was waiting for him in the van. "Today you start learning about the drama of the antique business," he said. "We're going to a furniture auction."

Jeremiah hopped into the van and rolled down the window.

"What do you do at an auction?"

"Usually, I buy some and sell some. Today, we're just going to buy. There's a lot to learn about auctions. It's easy to get caught up in the bidding and pay too much for something. You'll learn."

"You're going to let me bid?"

"Of course. You bid on the things you want to work on. Buy wisely, J.S. You know how hard it is to restore some old broken-down thing. Think about the blisters you're going to get, scraping and sanding. Every hour you spend eats into the profit."

Jeremiah knew what Bill was talking about. He had helped with dozens of projects and it was hard work.

"How will I know how much to pay? Besides that, I don't have any money."

"How does this deal sound? We'll pay for what you buy with

company money. You get to keep the profit when we sell it."

"That sounds good to me."

Bill stopped at a traffic light and downshifted.

"But there's a catch."

"You're always doing that to me, Bill."

"You have to put half of all you make into a savings account for an education fund. What's left over is yours to spend."

"You'll help me, won't you?"

"Sure. We'll help each other. That's how a partnership works."

They parked in the lot beside a large building. It had been the warehouse for a factory that was no longer in business. There was a big sign that read: *Eastern Indiana Furniture Auction*. License plates on the trucks parked there were from several states.

"First you have to get a bidding number." Bill told the clerk that they were from Loker and Stokely Antiques. The clerk gave them two cards with big red numbers. Bill's number was ninety-four and Jeremiah's was ninety-five.

"When you bid on something you hold up your number, so if you get it, they know who to charge," Bill explained.

The auctioneer began his rapid-fire chant. A large group of people gathered in front of him. It took Jeremiah a few minutes to understand what the man was saying.

Jeremiah studied Bill as he bid on a dilapidated desk and chair. The bid started at ten dollars and it didn't take long for the bidding to reach twenty.

Suddenly the auctioneer said, "*Sold* to number ninety-four!" Bill had bought the desk and chair for twenty-two dollars and fifty cents.

"It's your turn, J.S.," Bill told him. "Have you seen anything you'd like to bid on?"

"I think I'll bid on that old bookcase when it comes up," he whispered. "How high should I go?"

"Ah, J.S. That's the secret of this business. You have to get a feel for that sort of thing. My advice is to not get carried away. I always stop one bid below what I really want to pay for something."

Jeremiah took a closer look at the bookcase. It was covered with several coats of peeling paint. He tested its sturdiness and checked it for

any deep dents or gouges. Except that it was so ugly, it seemed to be in good condition.

The auctioneer's helper pointed at the bookcase and started the bidding. The auctioneer went into his chant. Two other people were bidding, and the auctioneer looked first at one bidder, then the other.

"Five dollars," Jeremiah said.

"Five, five, five, I gotta five—lemme hear a six—do I have a six?" the auctioneer chanted.

A card went up on the far side of the auction ring.

"Yesss, I got a six, anybody a seven, gotta six, want a seven, seven, seven, anybody a seven? Seven?"

"Seven," Jeremiah shouted, holding up his card. The palms of his hands were sweaty and he twisted his number card nervously. The higher it got, the less he wanted it. In fact, he hoped someone would outbid him. He watched Bill's smiling face as he bid. At least Bill was enjoying it.

Jeremiah studied the other bidders and wondered how high they would go. He didn't want to pay too much on the first thing he ever bid on.

The bidding was up to thirteen dollars. "Gotta thirteen, thirteen, do I have a fourteen? Fourteen, anybody? Anybody once. Anybody twice," the auctioneer pleaded.

"Fourteen," said Jeremiah.

"Gotta fourteen, fourteen, do I have a fifteen? Fifteen, anybody? Anybody once. Anybody twice, "the auctioneer sang.

"Sold!" the auctioneer shouted, "To number ninety-five."

The buyers turned their attention to an old oak dining table and Jeremiah sighed in relief as he went to inspect his purchase. He thought that even if he couldn't sell it, he could take it home to store his *National Geographic*s.

Bill bought a few more small items, then they left for home. They unloaded their purchases and carried them into the shop. Ruth called, "You men come up here right now and eat lunch. Don't get started on anything."

Jeremiah followed Bill up the short flight of stairs that led to the kitchen.

"Did you buy anything, Jeremiah?" Ruth asked.

"I got a bookcase for fourteen dollars." Jeremiah washed his hands.

Bill sat down at the table. "He bought it right, too. It'll take a lot of work, but it'll sell."

Ruth put a bowl of vegetable soup and a toasted cheese sandwich in front of each of them. "I haven't seen your mom for a few days. What's she up to?" She returned to the table with big slices of apple pie.

"She's going to take some pictures of the Sink today for Charlie Willig. Then he's taking us to dinner."

"Hmmm, is that the nice man she's been telling me about?"

"Uh huh. He was over at our house yesterday."

"Over at your house? Really?" Ruth smiled.

⧆ ⧆ ⧆

After lunch, Bill did the paperwork on their purchases, and Jeremiah found a space to start working on his bookcase.

"I cut out some more bird house parts for you," Bill remarked. "I also made the parts for a bat house. Bats ought to like the Sink. The last time I was there the bugs nearly drove me nuts."

"Lots of bugs there," Jeremiah agreed.

Jeremiah found a brush and opened a gallon of paint stripper. The sharp chemical odor pierced his nostrils and made his eyes water. He switched on the exhaust fan and went back to work, covering every surface of the bookcase with the thick, gooey substance.

"Don't get it on your skin. Burns to beat the band," Bill warned.

Jeremiah leaned against the table saw and watched as layers of paint bubbled and loosened. "Did I tell you that they've marked a bunch of trees in the Sink? They're going to cut them down."

"Who's doing that?"

"The county hired some tree guys, I guess. They want to dredge Hog Creek. Charlie is rushing to get the state to take over the place before it gets all messed up."

"It's a shame. We shouldn't be destroying what little wilderness is left."

"Charlie will save it."

"You know what Henry said, don't you? 'The wilderness is the promise of the future.'"

"Charlie says some people won't be happy until all the wild places are paved." Jeremiah looked for a piece of newspaper to wipe the paint remover from his brush. "I have a game at five-thirty. I'll need to leave here in about an hour. My bike has a flat so I have to walk, and Mom said I have to take a bath first."

"She probably told you to put on clean underwear, too."

"How did you know that?"

"Mothers have been telling their sons that since we first walked out of the caves. If I get around to it, I'll sort out some more wood for bird houses. Maybe we'll put some more of them together to-morrow."

"Hey, Bill. You're really getting into this bird house thing," Jeremiah teased. Then he started the hard work of scraping the sticky old paint off his new investment.

※ ※ ※

Jeremiah left the shop at four. When he got to the ball field, Brad was already unloading equipment from Coach McLean's van.

"Hey, Stokely. Come help carry stuff."

Jeremiah grabbed a bat bag and the catcher's equipment. He dragged them into the dugout and squatted by the bench.

"You look tired, Stokely. What's the matter? Spending too much time with Stacy?"

"You're such a jerk, Brad."

This game was different from the last two they played. The teams were evenly matched and by the end of the fifth inning, nei-ther team had scored. Jeremiah was at shortstop, Brad played sec-ond base, and Jerry Goldberg was at first, Todd's old position. Jeremiah, Brad and Todd had spent hours practicing their double-play routine. Jerry wasn't nearly the first baseman that Todd had been.

The first batter in the sixth inning singled to right field. With a runner on first, they were set up for a double play. The next batter swung on the first pitch and missed it by a mile. He took the next two balls. Jeremiah looked up to see Charlie helping Nina into the stands. This was the first game his mother had come to see since he played tee-ball in the second grade!

The batter got a piece of the next pitch. The ball took an odd hop just in front of the pitcher's mound and Jeremiah scrambled to get it. He rifled the ball to Brad at second, just as they had practiced. One out! Brad made a perfect throw to first, but Jerry was so far off the bag he dropped the ball getting back. Todd never would have dropped that ball.

Harry Sloan walked the next batter. Now, with runners on first and second, the crowd came alive. Fans for both teams jumped to their feet, cheering. Jeremiah glanced at the bleachers. Charlie and his mother were in deep conversation and had missed the excitement.

The next batter bunted, but Harry got the ball and threw the runner out at first. Still, this advanced the runners to second and third. Brad moved off the bag toward first base. Jeremiah moved closer to second. The crowd was screaming now.

Harry went into his windup. The pitch. The crack of the bat. Jason Swift snagged the ball after one hop in left field and relayed it to Jeremiah. Jeremiah made the throw to home plate, but too late. One run scored. Runners were still at second and third.

Coach McLean signaled Harry. The batter coming to the plate had a reputation of being dangerous. Jeremiah just knew he'd homer and empty the bases.

The crowd kept up its chant. Jeremiah tugged at his cap with a sweaty hand. He looked at Brad, who kicked at the dirt to get a solid foothold.

Harry concentrated on the batter. The first pitch was a called strike, the second one a swing and a miss. The third pitch was fouled down the third base line. Harry took his time. He pitched a fast ball right down the middle. Jeremiah saw it coming and expected to see the ball fly out of sight over the fence.

He was wrong. The batter swung and missed, retiring the sides. Jeremiah's team had survived the onslaught, but they were one run behind. As he walked toward the dugout, Jeremiah saw Harry's father cheering from the stands. He was the man with the moustache at the Sink with Linebacker. He didn't look nearly so mean as he had in the Sink.

Jeremiah was second in the batting order this inning. Harry walked. Jeremiah strolled to the batter's box. The crowd shouted encouragement. Brad yelled, "C'mon, Stokely, you can do it!"

Jeremiah glanced toward the stands as he tapped the bottom of his shoe with the bat. His mother and Charlie were still sitting there talking, not watching him at all.

The first pitch was high. Ball one.

"That's lookin' at 'em," Brad yelled.

From the corner of his eye, he could see his mom and Charlie.

Jeremiah thought the second pitch was too low and didn't swing. The umpire shouted, "Strike one." Jeremiah straightened and glared at the umpire.

He swung at the next pitch and fouled it down the first baseline.

"That's getting a piece of it, Stokely," Brad shouted.

The next pitch was high. The count was two and two.

Jeremiah took his stance and concentrated. The ball came hurtling toward him. He swung too late and too low. "You're *out*!" the umpire shouted.

Jeremiah trudged back to the bench. The next two batters did no better, and the tying run died on first. Neither team scored in the next three innings. The game ended with a one-to-nothing loss for Jeremiah's team.

Jeremiah helped Brad load the equipment into the coach's van.

"I should have hit that pitch," Jeremiah said.

"Hey, we'll get 'em in the playoffs."

Jeremiah was relieved. Brad wasn't always that forgiving. Only a few weeks ago, he had turned Jeremiah in to the authorities for keeping Spot in a cage.

Jeremiah walked to where his mother and Charlie still sat in the bleachers.

"Too bad, hon," Nina said. "It was a good game, though." She put her hand on his shoulder. Jeremiah had the urge to pull away. Instead he just stood there and stared at his beat-up shoes.

How would she know? She didn't see it. If she says, 'It matters not whether you win or lose, but how you play the game,' I'll never speak to her again, he thought.

"Are you hungry?" Charlie asked.

"I don't know about Jeremiah, but I'm starved," Nina said.

"I need to go home to change clothes," Jeremiah muttered.

"Okay," Charlie said, "Let's go."

◈ ◈ ◈

All the way home, Charlie and Nina talked and laughed about their picture-taking expedition. It was as if Jeremiah wasn't even in the car.

What's going on here? Jeremiah wondered. Yet he knew the answer. Rita had said, "Charlie thinks a lot of you and your mother." Then there was the way Ruth had said "Really?" when Jeremiah told her Charlie had visited them.

Maybe I should just say to Mom, 'Charlie is my friend, not yours.' His insides told him it wasn't that simple. Grownups! He shook his head in disgust.

Charlie and Nina waited in the car. Jeremiah changed his clothes fast and climbed back into the backseat. Charlie headed to the Hermitage.

"I called for reservations," Charlie said.

"You really don't have to do this, Charlie," Nina said.

"Hey, I want to. It isn't often that a person gets to have dinner with two of his favorite people in the whole world," Charlie said.

Two favorite people? Yeah, sure, Jeremiah thought.

Jeremiah ordered shrimp, fries and a Coke. The food was good, but Jeremiah felt left out of the conversation. They talked about the Sink and the pictures, but somehow it wasn't the same Sink where he and Stacy had sat in the sycamore.

◈ ◈ ◈

They got home at nine o'clock. Nina invited Charlie in for a cup of coffee, but he said, "Next time," and drove off. Jeremiah went straight to his room. He stretched out on his bed and put on the earphones. He didn't even bother to change the disk; he just listened to his mother's blues disk again.

Sleep didn't come. Maybe he should have written his dad yesterday as he always had on Sundays. Even if his letters wouldn't be delivered, there was always hope as long as he kept trying.

He picked up his nature journal and leafed through the first few pages. It was filling up with drawings and notes just like Audubon's. He flipped to the back of the book. Here he was keeping lists of the plants and animals he had seen in the Sink. He had already identified twelve different birds and nine kinds of trees. He held the edge of the book toward his face and found the exact middle. He opened it, bent the book backward to stretch the spine, and got a pen from the clutter on his nightstand. He wrote on the centerfold in large block letters:

LETTERS TO MY FATHER, STANLEY STOKELY

He turned the page and wrote:

Dear Dad,

You don't get my letters anymore, but I just had to write anyway. I'll keep what I write in this book. Maybe someday we will see each other and I'll give you the book. The first part is my nature journal. You don't have to read that.

I don't know what to do. When I thought I knew your address, I felt better, even if you didn't answer.

One time I took a map of the United States and drew a line from East Newport to Eugene, Oregon. Then I figured out how far it was. You know, I took the little mileage numbers and added them all together. I even looked up some of the towns along the way and made out like I had taken a bus to see you. It made me feel like we were connected because I could see that line on the map.

Do you remember when you showed me how to make a telephone with two tin cans and a piece of string? I pretended I had a can with a string a thousand miles long, and you had a can tied to it on the other end.

Now I don't know where you are, and that dream isn't any good anymore. I can't seem to come up with another one.

There are a lot of things bothering me right now. My friend Charlie is trying hard to get a state park going near here. Stacy and I have been taking bird houses there. Bill says it's important to save the Sink because of the plants and animals. He thinks we can't have a good world for people if it isn't a good world for all living things.

I saw on TV that in Oklahoma there is a place where they have made a huge park and let the prairie grass grow back for the buffalo.

That's what Charlie is trying to do. He wants to put the Sink back like it was. It's not big enough for buffalo, but there are already lots of animals and birds there. Some tree guys chased me away from the Sink. Charlie says it's because they think they will lose money if it's a park.

Charlie is a very nice man. He likes Mom and me a lot. Mom took pictures for him and that makes her happy.

I miss Todd a lot. I'm going to go see him, but I don't know when. I keep wishing he would call me. Mom says we can't afford to call him.

That's all I can think of this time.

Your son,
Jeremiah Stokely, Naturalist

He reread the letter. His eye fell on the part where he said that Charlie is a nice man. He knew this wasn't what he really wanted to say. Sure, Charlie was a nice man, but now he knew the reason he just had to write this letter. It was because he thought Charlie was a little *too* nice—to his mother. Why hadn't he said that in the letter? Maybe it seemed too much like tattling, even though his dad would never see the letter. He couldn't get it out of his mind.

He put the book on the bedside table and twisted his neck to see the alarm clock. Eleven thirty-six. He wasn't sleepy, so he took off the earphones and went downstairs to get a bowl of cereal.

The moon had been full three nights before. It was smaller now, but in a nearly cloudless sky, it cast eerie shadows. He ate his cereal and started out the back door. The horse chestnut in the vacant lot next door was surrounded by a halo.

He closed the door without banging it and walked toward the tree. The knee-high grass was damp from yesterday's storm. It smelled fresh, and the crickets stopped singing as he passed.

It had often been a place where he went to think. It had been his camp when he was little and pretended to be Great Thunder, an Indian buffalo hunter. He leaned his head against the trunk. The buffalo had seemed so real then.

The moon slipped behind a thin cloud. *There are no buffalo*, he told himself. *There are no tin can telephones with thousand-mile strings. Get real!*

CHAPTER EIGHT

Nina had breakfast on the table when Jeremiah struggled down the stairs. He yawned. Even after his trip to the horse chestnut tree he didn't sleep well. He had one confusing dream after another.

"I sure didn't sleep well last night," he said, squelching another yawn.

His mother hugged him. "I had the same problem. I guess it was all the excitement. Yesterday was a good day, wasn't it?"

"We lost the game."

"Yeah, you did," she said. She set a glass of orange juice in front of him. "I was watching you at dinner last night. Something is bothering you. Are you going to tell me, or do I start guessing and embarrass us both?"

"What do you mean?"

"I mean, I can always tell. You think you're so cool, and you keep things inside. You think I don't know, but I do. I even know why you do it."

"Okay, why?"

"You do it to protect me. You think I already have so much to worry about that when things are troubling you, you don't tell me. How's that for starters?"

"Could be." Jeremiah stared at the table. He didn't dare let his eyes come into contact with his mother's.

"I'm that way, too. I guess it's in your genes." She patted his hand.

She was right. Jeremiah always had some secret he was planning to spring on her when the time was right. He hadn't told her about the bookcase. He hadn't told her that he was worried about the way she smiled at Charlie and the way Charlie looked back at her.

"I don't suppose we'll ever be any different, Jeremiah. We could try, though—communicating more, I mean."

"I guess."

"I'll take the film to the camera shop before work today. The pictures should be ready Thursday."

"Can you give me enough money to get the tire fixed on my bike?"

"Bring me my purse. You need a haircut, too."

※ ※ ※

Jeremiah pushed his bike down the alley to the shop. Not having his bike for one day had messed up his routine. Every day since he first discovered the Sink, he had found time to go there. Sometimes it was for only a few minutes, just long enough to write a few notes in his journal. Other times, Stacy went along and they stayed longer, to sit in their tree or see how many birds they could identify. The tire looked pretty bad. He wasn't sure if he could repair it or if he needed a new one. His mother had given him her last ten-dollar bill. If he had to get a new tire, there wouldn't be enough to get a haircut.

He pulled off his cap and looked at his hair in the reflection in the shop door. *I can get by without a haircut,* he thought.

No sooner had he opened the door than Bill shouted, "Be sure you measure yourself, J.S. You may be in for a surprise."

Jeremiah didn't know what joke Bill was trying to pull, but he dutifully stood up to the tape Bill had attached to the doorsill. As always, he compared his height to the mark that showed how tall he was when he was nine. Then he looked up at the mark at six-foot-one, Bill's height.

"Are you six-foot-two, J.S.?"

"Yeah, sure, Bill."

"Well, if you aren't, you ought to feel like it. Let me show you what I found."

Bill had Jeremiah's bookcase on a workbench and held a magnifying glass over a little copper plate on the bottom shelf.

"I wasn't paying attention to what you were doing yesterday. I came in early this morning to see how things were progressing. I discovered something that intrigued me. Look here."

He handed Jeremiah the magnifier. "I thought it might be mission oak, but I was wrong. What do you see?"

Jeremiah focused the magnifier on the small metal plate. It had an emblem engraved in it, but it meant nothing to him. "It's just got some kind of a symbol on it. Does it mean something?"

"It means that you are one lucky duck," Bill said. He handed Jeremiah an antique catalog open to a page that had photographs of several bookcases like the one on the bench. "It's an original Roycroft, J.S."

"Is that good?" Jeremiah studied the photos and found one exactly like his bookcase.

"Good? Look at the suggested book price for this thing." Bill ran his stubby finger down the page. "What does this say?"

"Ninety-five dollars? You mean this little bookcase is worth ninety-five dollars?"

"Read it again, J. S. This time put the decimal point in the right place."

Jeremiah looked at the listed price. He still thought something was wrong. "It says here nine hundred and fifty dollars. That can't be right."

"Right as rain, J.S.! You have discovered what keeps all antique buffs going back for more, a diamond in the rough. With all that ugly paint, no one recognized it. This is a valuable piece of furniture."

"Can we really sell it for that much?"

"Might be able to get even more. It depends on how eager some collector is to have it."

"Wow!" Jeremiah looked at the catalog again. It showed the Roycroft emblem and described the copper plate. He studied the plate on the bookcase again to make sure it was a match. Convinced that they were the same, he dropped the magnifier on the bench and did a war dance like a tight-end who had just crossed into the end zone after a fifty-five yard run. "Yesss!"

"Well, how tall do you feel?"

"Six-foot-two!"

"You'll want to be very careful so you don't damage the wood," Bill warned. He opened his pocketknife and carefully scraped the back of the top shelf. "I swear, J.S., it looks to me like it is in fine shape under all that paint."

"Do you think I'll be able to get all the old paint off?"

"This is not something you can rush, J.S." Bill put the bookcase back on the floor. "You'll need to go over it several times. You remember how we did that old dresser a while back?"

"Let it dry out between each coat of finish remover, right?"

"That's part of it. Details are important. Making sure you get into all the corners and tight places is what makes you a professional. I'll inspect your work from time to time."

Jeremiah knew he really had his work cut out for him, but all the effort was going to pay off—big. He gathered a putty knife, a scraper and a handful of newspapers to catch the old bubbled-up paint.

▩ ▩ ▩

As the day wore on, Jeremiah realized he hadn't underestimated the labor involved. He was very careful. He didn't want to take any chances with his rare find.

"That catalog said this is Roycroft furniture. What does that mean?"

"For one thing, it means it's older than we thought. Probably made around the turn of the century near Buffalo, New York."

"Buffalo, huh?" Jeremiah smiled. Just last night he had convinced himself that buffalo existed only in his imagination. Now the word took on an entirely different meaning.

At lunchtime, Bill brought sandwiches. Jeremiah stopped long enough to eat and went right back to his task. While the work occupied his hands, his mind was free to wander. He thought about the camera he had put on layaway at Phil's Camera Shop. It had been several weeks since he invested the seventy dollars to hold the Nikon.

He had almost given up on saving the six hundred thirty dollars he still owed and feared he might even lose his deposit. He had done that foolish thing when he thought he would have a steady income for the summer. Then all his plans evaporated. He tried the fish bait business, but the earthworms died in the basement. He'd tried a lawn mowing service, but had only one customer. His gadget manufacturing business had bogged down.

Now his spirits grew with each sticky glob of paint he scraped from the bookcase. He fought the urge to calculate the day when he would make the final payment on the camera. *But like Bill says, 'Don't count your chickens before the eggs have hatched.' We still have to find a buyer,* Jeremiah thought.

Except for the occasional whine of a power tool, the shop was silent. By mid-afternoon the bare wood began to show through the paint. Bill called for break-time.

"J.S., go get us some pop, and there are cookies on the counter."

Jeremiah wiped his hands on a pink shop towel, as he had seen Bill do hundreds of times, and went to the refrigerator. He returned with their snacks.

"Mom fixed me a Louisiana breakfast Sunday morning."

"Oh, she did? What brought that on?"

"Well, I told her that the Sink looks like a Louisiana bayou. It does, too. I found pictures in a *National Geographic.*"

"Your grandpa really liked the bayou country. Your grandparents came to see me when I was down south. I guess your mom was four or five at the time. Maybe you inherited your grandpa's love of swamps. We went fishing with a Cajun friend of mine. Really had a good time. I have a picture someplace of your mom in a straw hat, holding a fishing pole. I ought to dig out those old pictures some time."

"What does 'Cajun' mean?"

"It's a corruption of the word Acadian. A long time ago, French people were forced out of Canada. Many of them ended up in Louisiana. Their families mixed with other people there, and now they call themselves Cajun. It's quite a rich culture."

"Mom played some of their music for me."

"Arthur Fowler, Joseph's dad, studied the traditional music of

Louisiana and wrote several scholarly papers about it." Bill ran his hand over Jeremiah's bookcase. "I don't think the wood has dried enough to start sanding, J.S. But you're doing a good job."

"Maybe we could put some houses together while it's drying," Jeremiah said. He mashed their cola cans in the can crusher and pitched them into the recycling bin.

"I need to leave some time to get my tire fixed. Mom told me to get a haircut, too, but I don't need one. Do you think I need one?" Jeremiah picked up the pieces of a bird house and clamped them together like Bill had shown him.

"You're not dragging me into that argument. Here, let me hold the top until you get the nails started."

"I was talking to Joseph Fowler the other day and he said that you and his dad had been friends all the way back to your college days. I didn't know you went to college," Jeremiah said as he wielded the hammer.

"There are a lot of things you don't know about me, J.S."

Jeremiah finished the bird house and lifted the parts for a bat house onto the workbench. He found the right size of screws in one of the little plastic hardware drawers.

"It was actually your grandfather who introduced Arthur Fowler to me. Arthur's dad ran the bait shop where your grandfather went. And it was one of those magic times. As soon as we shook hands, it was like we had always known each other. We knew right away that we would always be friends."

"Joseph said it was because of you that they moved here."

Bill looked admiringly at the finished bat house, placed it beside the bird house on the floor and picked up another set of pre-cut house parts.

"I guess I had a hand in it. Arthur had studied at a black college, and because of the times, he had a hard time getting a good job."

"What do you mean?"

"Arthur applied for a position at the university, but there was a white applicant, too. It looked like the white guy was going to get the job, not because he was more talented, but just because he was white."

"So why does Joseph say that they moved here because of you? Just because you're friends?"

"Well, I knew both these people and Arthur was by far the better choice. I put in a good word for him and he got the job."

"But didn't that make your white friend mad?" Jeremiah said in a puzzled voice.

"Not at all, I was looking for an excuse to leave the university and take up woodworking anyway," Bill said.

"The other guy was you? Are you crazy? Didn't you want the job?"

"Sure, I wanted it. It was a good job and I could have done it. But I didn't want to get the job just because I was white. And, I didn't want Arthur not to get it just because he's black."

Jeremiah shook his head in disbelief. "That's when you started the shop?"

"That's right, and it's been a beautiful life for me and for Arthur." Bill smiled. "Your grandfather used to say, 'Talent is not at *all* like beauty.' There's a lesson to be learned there."

"Like what?"

"Hey, do I have to explain everything to you? I'm going up to rest for a while. You think about it while you do your errands and tell me what your grandfather meant by that."

※ ※ ※

Jeremiah pushed his bike to Arnold's Sports Store. All the way Jeremiah tried to think what Bill was talking about. *Talent is not at all like beauty. What kind of a lesson is that?* he wondered. It wasn't until he parked his bike outside the sports store that it hit him. *Beauty is skin-deep, but talent isn't. So that's what my grandfather meant!*

Arnold's was the only complete sporting goods shop in town. The store sold everything from baseball cards to canoes. Every time he went by there and saw the yellow canoe in the window he thought about Todd and Pigeon River.

He got a used tire for two-fifty and Arnold helped him put it on. The barbershop was just around the corner and Jeremiah was the only customer, so he got right into the chair.

The barber wanted to talk, but Jeremiah couldn't get the book-case off his mind.

He was back at work in less than an hour and a half. Bill was still napping, so Jeremiah worked alone the rest of the afternoon and locked up about four-thirty.

※ ※ ※

Jeremiah left home early the next morning to go to the Sink before going to the shop. Even though he was a little late, Bill still didn't have the shop open. Jeremiah let himself in with his key and went right to work. He selected fine-grit sandpaper and concentrated on his job. He knew to always sand with the grain of the wood, not across it.

About ten-thirty Ruth came to the shop. "Bill's not feeling well today, Jeremiah. He said to tell you to go ahead with what you're doing. There may be a UPS delivery. If it comes, just bring the receipt up and I'll sign it, okay?"

"What's the matter with Bill?"

"Oh, he'll be okay. Just tired. He'll be up and about later. Nothing to worry about. If you get hungry, come up. I'll fix you something."

She left Jeremiah in the quiet of the shop. He always felt strange when he was there alone.

It started to rain. First it was just oblong splotches on the front window. In a few minutes it was a downpour—a "goose drownder," Bill would call it. That meant Jeremiah's game would be rained out. He wouldn't have another one until Friday. By then, he should have the bookcase finished and ready to sell.

Jeremiah's work was progressing so well that he felt it was safe to count a few chickens. He went to Bill's desk and found a pencil and a long yellow tablet of paper.

He wrote "Sale of bookcase—$950." Under that he wrote "Cost of bookcase—$14" and subtracted. Bill hadn't said anything about the cost of getting the bookcase ready to sell. Jeremiah knew that finish remover was expensive and he had used nearly a gallon. He decided it was only right to subtract that cost, too. Also, he had used several sheets of sandpaper already. Then there was the varnish that he and Bill would put on the bookcase. Jeremiah estimated that the total expense would be about twenty dollars. That left nine hundred sixteen dollars.

He looked at the figure for a long time before he did the next step. He had to save half of that amount—four hundred fifty-eight dollars.

He threw the pencil down. "That's not enough," he said.

"What's not enough, Jeremiah?" Ruth asked. She was standing at the kitchen door, wiping her hands on a dishtowel.

"Oh, nothing. I was just trying to figure something out."

"I fixed some soup and sandwiches. Would you like to eat?"

"Is Bill up yet?"

"He was up for a little. He has a doctor's appointment tomorrow morning. Come on up?"

Jeremiah's face dropped. Bill was never sick. "He's going to be all right, isn't he?"

"I'm sure he will."

❖ ❖ ❖

The afternoon dragged without Bill. Jeremiah wished he were there. He didn't want to make any mistakes. He thought he had the bookcase sanded just right and was anxious to brush on the finish. But he wouldn't start without Bill's advice.

He found a sheet of the finest grit of sandpaper in the shop and went over every surface of the bookcase again.

The mantel clock struck four. He swept up the fine dust the sanding had left on the floor, turned on the shop vac and cleaned every crevice on the bookcase.

When he went to tell Ruth that UPS hadn't come, Bill was still sleeping.

"Tell Bill I figured out my grandfather's lesson. Tell him that beauty may be skin-deep, but talent has nothing to do with skin."

"Will Bill know what that means?"

Jeremiah smiled and nodded, and then he locked up the shop.

He saw his mother picking up the mail as he rested his bike against the porch.

"How was your day?" she asked.

"Bill's sick."

"I know. I talked to Ruth on the phone today."

Jeremiah felt a tug in his stomach. "He's never sick. What's wrong?"

"Ruth didn't say. I'm sure he'll be okay. Let's have some supper. You set the table."

Jeremiah moved Nina's photography books to one corner of the table and set two places. "Bill told me that he had a picture of you and Grandpa fishing in Louisiana."

"He probably does. I don't remember that trip. Sometimes I think I do, but then I think it's only because Dad talked about it so much. He really liked the Gulf Coast. He and Mom thought about moving there. That's where their accident happened, you know."

Jeremiah didn't know. *How could I know? Bill is the only one who tells me anything. If Bill dies* . . . His thought trailed off. It was too horrible to even consider. He began to feel the hair on the back of his neck creep. He tried not to let his anger—his fear—show.

They had cheeseburgers because his mother had brought home day-old buns. She had also brought a butterscotch pie that had a damaged crust and couldn't be sold.

"Charlie came by the store today. He asked about you. He has everything ready to take to the Department of Natural Resources office in Indianapolis except the pictures. I told him you would bring them to me Thursday."

"Sure. What time?"

"The camera shop said they'll be ready by early afternoon. Oh, I hope they're good."

"They'll be good, Mom. Just wait and see. They'll be great."

"Jeremiah," Nina began. She got up from the table and walked to the sink with her cup. "You remember when I said I thought we should be more open with each other?"

"Sure." Jeremiah tilted his glass a little too far and milk dribbled down his chin. He wondered if Bill had said something to tip off his mother about his secret.

"Oh, Jeremiah, look at you. Here!" She threw Jeremiah a towel. "When Charlie was in the store today, he asked me to go to a blues festival next week. Sort of a celebration for getting his proposal done. How would you feel about that?"

Jeremiah felt a vibration go up his spine and leave a hollow feeling in his stomach. He cleared his throat.

"You mean, like a date?"

"Well, not exactly a date, but—yes, like a date. It's in Indianapolis. Ruth said you could stay there until we got back."

"But Charlie is *my* friend."

"I know he is, sweetie. He's also my friend. Would you want me to be with someone who wasn't your friend?"

"Oh, Mom. You know what I mean."

"Well, he did take both of us out to eat. But you wouldn't enjoy the concert. What do you think?"

"Is he going to be a part of our team now?"

"What a strange thing to ask, Jeremiah," Nina said.

CHAPTER NINE

Jeremiah's baseball card collection had slid off his cluttered dresser during the night and wedged itself between the door and the box that held his rock collection. He tugged at the door, but it wouldn't open. He heard his mother up and moving around the kitchen.

He finally dislodged the baseball cards, moved the box and pulled the door open. Todd's handcuffs jingled against the door.

Nina was savoring the aroma of a freshly brewed cup of coffee as Jeremiah entered the kitchen.

"Good morning, sweetheart," she said. She grabbed Jeremiah and planted a noisy kiss on his cheek.

"Oh, Mom, stop that."

"I'm taking some time off after you bring me the pictures. Don't forget, now. Charlie is coming by to select the ones he wants to use. I'll have to make up the time this afternoon."

"I won't forget, Mom. I know the guys at Phil's Camera Shop. Gilbert Paxon's my friend."

"How do you know Gilbert?" Nina's puzzled expression caught Jeremiah off guard.

He drew a deep breath and stammered. "Er—I just know him." He didn't dare tell his mother that it was Gilbert who had shown him a certain Nikon dozens of times. It was Gilbert who had let him put the camera on layaway, Gilbert who had signed the receipt for seventy dollars to hold the camera.

"Would you like some eggs?" Nina asked.

Jeremiah pulled a box of corn flakes from the cupboard, found a bowl and filled it with cereal. He poured milk on it. "This will be okay."

"You haven't said much lately about what you and Bill are doing in the shop."

He swallowed hard. "I'm working on a bookcase. Bill says I can have the profit from the furniture I work on."

"Ruth told me you guys had cooked up some deal."

"He says I have to save half of the money for education."

"That's a good idea," his mother said. She turned her eyes to the window. Her voice was soft and far away. "It won't be long before we'll have to start thinking about that."

Jeremiah finished his breakfast and started to wash his bowl.

"I'll get the dishes, hon. Did you make your bed?"

"Sort of."

"You go on, then. I'll finish up here. Please bring me the pictures at Mason's as soon as you can. By the way, the spring on the back door is broken. Do you think Bill would have a replacement?"

"I'll ask." Jeremiah slapped his baseball cap onto his head. He leaped off the porch and grabbed his bike. He had enough time to make a run to the Sink before going to the shop.

❖ ❖ ❖

Even with his side trip, he arrived at the shop earlier than expected. He had his key poised to unlock the door, but it was open. He went in and was surprised to see Bill already at work.

"I thought you'd be at the doctor, Bill."

"I felt so much better this morning, I decided not to go."

Ruth was standing in the kitchen doorway. "Against my better judgment. See if you can talk some sense into his stubborn old head, Jeremiah."

"Now, Ruth, I'm fine," Bill said. He raised his left hand and motioned for her to go away.

"Don't expect any sympathy from me if you're down in bed again tomorrow, William Loker."

Bill laughed. "Ruthy, Ruthy, Ruthy."

Ruth didn't like to be called "Ruthy." She spun around, slammed the door and disappeared.

"Good news, J.S. I talked to Jake Nathan over in Ohio about your bookcase. He's really interested. He said he'd come over tomorrow morning to take a look. You know, of course, that *you've* got to close the deal."

"Me? I don't know how to do that." Jeremiah had watched Bill dozens of times as he dickered with customers about the price of a piece of furniture, but . . .

"You know how much the catalog says it's worth. What you have to decide is how much you're willing to sell it for. I want you to drive a hard bargain. If Jake wants it, he'll take it as is. He likes to put the final finish on himself. Doesn't trust anyone else."

Jeremiah looked at the bookcase. "I still can't believe that anyone would pay a lot of money for it. It's just an ugly old thing."

Bill picked up a piece of used sandpaper. "Let's put a coat of sanding sealer on it. When it's dry, you can sand it all over again."

It went on more easily than the paint remover had. Bill had selected a small, soft-bristled brush for the job. They worked slowly and purposefully, taking great care to cover every inch of the surface.

After a long silence, during which the only sound in the shop was the ticking of the mantel clock, Jeremiah said, "You remember what you said about woodworking being a good thing to know?" Jeremiah put the brush into a can of brush cleaner and tightened the lid on the sanding sealer.

"I think there's something spiritual about it. To me it's more than a way of making a living."

"But you have a college education. You could have done other things."

"I did do other things. I just wanted to do what I love. Everyone ought to have that chance."

"That's what I think, too."

"You're thinking about your secret project, aren't you? You're right. She should have a chance to be a photographer."

"I could get Mom's camera out of layaway with this money."

"I knew that's what you had in mind," Bill said. He ran his hand over the top of the bookcase to check the smoothness. "Don't be disappointed if this doesn't all work out the way you've planned. "

Jeremiah wiped his hands. "I know—*Don't be too hasty*—you're always telling me that."

"Hand me that carton of steel wool, J.S." He took the box from Jeremiah.

Bill stood beside Jeremiah and they both admired the bookcase. "Now, back to selling this thing. Our buyer said he'd be here at nine-thirty tomorrow morning. Can I count on you to be here to collect your spoils? Reap the benefit of your harvest? Drive a hard bargain? Wheel and . . ."

"Okay, okay, I'll be here, but I do have a game at one o'clock."

"Well, if you haven't closed the deal by then, you'll never make it in this business. Let's put together some more bird houses before lunch."

◈ ◈ ◈

Ruth had made potato soup. Jeremiah helped with the dishes while Bill rested on the couch.

"Your mother said this is a big day. You know, getting the prints for her first real photography assignment," Ruth said.

"Yeah, Charlie has to have them at the DNR headquarters tomorrow."

"Charlie is such a nice person, don't you think?"

Jeremiah nodded without enthusiasm. He was beginning to regret he had volunteered his mother to take the pictures. Helping Charlie with the pictures was one thing, but going on a date with him was something else.

He looked at the grandfather clock beside the couch where Bill was sleeping soundly. "I think the pictures are probably ready by now. Maybe Bill will be awake by the time I get back," he said. He hung the dish towel over the edge of the counter.

"Jeremiah, you're a big help to Bill. I appreciate it a lot. You give him a reason to keep going."

"I thought it was the other way around."

"You're precious, Jeremiah."

⊞ ⊞ ⊞

On his way to the photo shop, Jeremiah stopped his bike in front of Arnold's Sports Store. The glare of the sun made him cup his hands to see the yellow canoe hanging in the window. Arnold was putting a baseball card display in front of it. He motioned Jeremiah inside.

"Have you given up on your baseball card collection, Jeremiah?"

"Not exactly."

"Well, you haven't been in for a while. I got a new bunch of Donruss you might like to look through. I know that's what you collect mostly."

"I've been doing other things. I still mess with them some."

"Just checking. You know where I am. Always ready to do business with you."

Jeremiah spent a moment looking at price tags on the new bikes parked on the sidewalk. He couldn't believe how expensive they were.

Phil's Camera Shop was two doors farther down. He leaned his bike against a fire zone sign and went in. Gilbert waved as Jeremiah entered.

"Want to look at your camera, Jeremiah?" Gilbert asked.

"I just wanted to tell you that I may be able to pay for it soon. I'll be so glad when my mom has a real, professional camera."

"Well, there are professional cameras and then there are professional cameras. Your camera is a start. But, look here." He opened a glass showcase and placed a large camera on a foam mat on the counter. "Here's what a real professional needs. It's a Hasselblad."

"How much does a camera like that cost?"

"Well, the camera body alone costs a minimum of two thousand dollars. Then there are lenses, extra film carriers and all the accessories in the world. You could spend a fortune on a camera like this before you ever took a single picture."

"Then my mother's Nikon isn't good enough?"

"I didn't say that."

Jeremiah was stunned. After all his work and planning he was not getting his mother the best camera after all and he hadn't known the difference. It made him think of the baseball mitt his mother had bought him. Maybe this was the same thing. Would his mother think the Nikon was a cheap imitation when she really needed a Hasselblad? Would she pretend the Nikon was okay when it wasn't? Would she be ridiculed by other professional photographers?

"I'm supposed to pick up some pictures," Jeremiah said as Gilbert replaced the gleaming camera.

"They just came in."

Gilbert sorted through the stacks of envelopes. "Here they are, Nina Stokely, three packages."

He went to the cash register. "I'm afraid we have a problem here, Jeremiah. None of the pictures turned out. There's no charge if they don't print, and not a one of them did."

"Don't kid around, Gilbert. Those pictures are important."

"Sorry to say, I'm not kidding. Look here." Gilbert opened one of the envelopes and showed Jeremiah the negatives. Jeremiah knew that they should be black but they were all a fuzzy gray. There wasn't an image on any of them.

"Your mom's camera must have leaked light. That happens sometimes."

"Oh, no! Mom's going to die."

Jeremiah grabbed the envelopes and ran from the store. It was eight blocks to Mason's and Jeremiah had never pedaled harder in his life. He took a shortcut down Vine Street and skidded around the corner onto Wysor. He turned down the alley and shot into Mason's parking lot from the rear. He didn't bother to park his bike. He jumped off while it was still moving, and it continued for a few feet and crashed into a stack of wooden shipping pallets.

He ran to his mother's cash register. She wasn't there. He saw a young woman stacking canned peaches on a shelf.

"Where's Nina Stokely?" he gasped.

"I think she's on break. Probably in the back room."

Jeremiah started to the rear of the store.

"Hey, kid. You can't go back there. It's employees only."

"I've got to see her. She's my mother."

"You wait here. I'll find her."

Jeremiah paced between the potato chips and the soft drinks. He stopped twice to look in the envelopes to see if Gilbert had been mistaken. Each time he looked, his stomach flip-flopped.

After what seemed an hour, his mother walked eagerly toward him.

"Jeremiah, I didn't expect you so soon," she said. "Let me see the pictures." Her hands shook with excitement.

Jeremiah felt the blood drain from his face. He couldn't tell her. He set his jaw and handed the packages to his mother.

She opened the first envelope. Her face fell as she sorted through the blank negatives. Her eyes filled with disbelief.

"They're no good! Every one of them is ruined. Oh, Jeremiah," she sobbed. She put her hands to her forehead. Her shoulders slumped. "What am I going to do? What will Charlie say?"

"Gilbert said that light must have gotten into the camera," Jeremiah said.

"It's those old things they loan to us students. Other people in my class have had trouble with them. I guess I've been lucky—until now. Oh, Jeremiah, I've got to call Charlie."

She left Jeremiah standing between the chips and the two-liter bottles of cola.

She returned, still shaking her head. She kept looking in the envelopes as if, the more she searched, the more chance she would find her wonderful pictures hidden inside.

"He's not at his office. He's probably on his way, expecting to pick out the pictures for his proposal. I failed, Jeremiah."

"You can take them again—with a better camera."

"There's no time. Charlie has to make his presentation at one o'clock tomorrow afternoon. He believes his proposal might not be approved without pictures."

"What do you want me to do?"

"You go on back to Bill's. I'll call you there after I've talked to Charlie."

"I'm sorry, Mom."

"Oh, thanks, sweetie," she sighed. She hugged him. "I've got to get to my register. I'll call."

Jeremiah retrieved his bike from its tangle behind the store. He started for the shop. He couldn't get the Hasselblad out of his mind. A Hasselblad would not have leaked light.

He had to wait for a train on Wysor Street. The rushing cars lifted whirls of dust in the air. The rhythmic beat of the wheels on the crossing was dreamlike. Had this been last week, he might have lapsed into a daydream in which he heroically saved the day and the pictures in the envelopes were masterpieces. This time, the wheels seemed to say, "No buffalo—buffalo—no tin can telephone—tin can telephone. Get real—get real." He stared blankly at the sides of the railroad cars.

❖ ❖ ❖

Bill was in the shop when Jeremiah returned.

"Bill, Mom's got a big problem. None of the pictures she took in the Sink are any good. The camera leaked light."

"That's a shame, J.S. Is she going to have to do them again?"

"There's no time. Charlie needs them tomorrow."

"That *is* a crisis."

"Mom's probably talking to Charlie right now. Maybe he'll know what to do."

"Well, what I do when I have a problem is work it off. Let's look at your bookcase. Tomorrow is your big day."

Ruth called from the top of the kitchen stairs, "Jeremiah, it's your mother."

Jeremiah wiped his hands on a shop towel and ran to the phone.

"Jeremiah, we may have a solution. I'm going to borrow a different camera. Charlie will take us to the Sink at sunrise and get some new shots."

"How will you get them developed?"

"There's a one-hour film lab in Indianapolis, close to where he'll make his proposal. You and I will get the film developed and take him the finished prints. While he's in his meeting, we'll go to the zoo. How does that sound?"

"Awright!" Jeremiah said, pumping one arm.

"I've asked for the day off tomorrow. I'll have to work late tonight and Saturday to make up for it. Can you stay with Bill and Ruth?"

He turned to Ruth. "Mom wants to know if I can stay until she gets here."

Ruth nodded. "Of course. Anytime."

Jeremiah was on the way back to the shop when it hit him. "Oh, no!"

"What's the matter, J.S.?" Bill looked up from his desk.

"I just told Mom I'd go to Indianapolis with her and Charlie tomorrow. I can't. The guy's coming from Ohio to look at the bookcase, and I have a game." Jeremiah sat down on the bottom step. "I could miss the game, but . . ."

"I could ask Jake to come another day."

"We can't do that, either. I've just got to get Mom's camera out of layaway right away. She wouldn't be in trouble if she had her own camera."

Bill smiled briefly and said, "Every problem brings new possibilities, J.S."

"I'll just have to stay home. Rats! Mom and I were going to the zoo." Under his breath he muttered, "Packleruma!"

※ ※ ※

After supper, Bill took the evening paper to the couch and was asleep in five minutes. Jeremiah helped with the dishes and played solitaire until Nina arrived at eleven-fifteen. Bill was still snoozing on the couch and Jeremiah was at the computer e-mailing Todd. When Jeremiah went to the kitchen, he overheard Ruth talking to his mother. He caught the last word, "Charlie," and then Ruth giggled.

"Oh, Ruth. Stop it, now," his mother said. She turned to Jeremiah. "Are you ready to go, partner? We have to be up at the crack of dawn."

"I can't go to Indianapolis with you."

"Why not, hon?"

"I have a game."

"Surely you can miss one game. Other kids miss from time to time. What happens when people go on vacation?"

"I just can't go, that's all."

"Well, we'll talk about it on the way home. Thanks for taking care of my kid, Ruth."

Bill stirred on the couch.

Jeremiah grabbed his cap and started for the door. "Thanks, Ruth. See you in the morning, Bill. For sure."

They left by the side door that led to the alley. It was a dark night and it took a few minutes for their eyes to adjust. Nina put her arm around her son's shoulder.

"I really think you should go with us tomorrow. Charlie is looking forward to a day together—just the three of us."

Jeremiah thought, *Yeah, sure, the three of us.* Instead he said, "I'll be okay, Mom. Besides, Bill needs me tomorrow, too."

"Well, at least you can go with us when we retake the pictures."

"Yeah, I'd like that." He thought of the dozens of fantasies in which he and his mother were up at dawn in some far-off land, taking pictures. But those daydreams were about the two of them, not the three of them.

He opened the back door for his mother. The night-light made her skin glow beneath her dark hair.

"If we only had the money, I'd buy my own camera," she said.

Jeremiah smiled to himself.

CHAPTER TEN

Five-thirty came too soon for Jeremiah. He hadn't slept well enough or long enough. Even so, he was sitting on the front porch before his mother was out of bed.

Nina opened the door. "You'd better come in for a little breakfast, hon."

"I had a glass of milk, Mom. I'll eat something before I go to the shop."

"Is something bothering you, Jeremiah?"

"I'm okay, Mom."

She sighed and closed the door.

It had been a long time since Jeremiah had been up so early. He liked the freshness of early summer mornings. Once he and Bill had gone fishing at Grand Lake over in Ohio. They had left East Newport at four in the morning, and Jeremiah had slept all the way there. He had a feeling that he wasn't going to get any more sleep today.

After a few minutes, Charlie arrived in a state-owned truck.

"Morning," he said, sitting on the step beside Jeremiah. "I hope we can all squeeze into the truck. My car is in the shop."

Nina returned to the porch. "Jeremiah thinks he can't go to Indy with us. He has an important game today."

"That's too bad, Jeremiah," Charlie said.

"Bill needs me today, too."

"Well, the only thing to do is plan a day when we can go to

Indianapolis and not be on an errand. We'll take a fun day, just the three of us."

There's that 'three of us' stuff again, Jeremiah thought.

"We'd better get started, Charlie. I don't want to miss any of the morning light," Nina said. Charlie and Jeremiah both reached for her camera bag.

"I'll carry it for you, Mom."

Charlie smiled at Jeremiah and let go. "Come on, you two. Let's go take pictures."

❖ ❖ ❖

The sun was creeping over the embankment by the time they got to Hog Creek. It cast long shadows across the water in the lake. The morning haze swirled in the breeze.

"This place is gorgeous, Charlie," Nina said. She lowered her bag and started clicking photos.

Nina stood at the foot of Jeremiah's sycamore. She cradled the camera in her hands and rested her elbows on the trunk. She focused on a clump of sycamore leaves that glowed yellow-green, lit from behind by the sun.

Jeremiah walked up the trunk and sat on his limb. He wished Stacy were sitting on hers.

Nina retraced her steps, remembering the shots she had taken before. At one point, she scooped up a handful of water and dropped it on the broad leaves of a plant that slanted over the water. She waited until the water stood in beads, sparkling like jewels in the morning sun. Then she clicked the shutter. Another time she spread out a sheet of plastic and lay on her stomach, her camera nearly on the ground to get just the right angle.

By seven-thirty, they were back in the truck, with Jeremiah in the middle, heading back to town.

"Jeremiah, this is the second time you've canceled an outing with us because of a game. If I ever coach a baseball team, I hope all my players are as dependable as you," Charlie said. "Imagine, giving up a trip to the zoo to play a game. I'm proud of you."

"I'm proud of you, too, hon. You be sure to eat some breakfast before you go to Bill's."

"You haven't had breakfast, Jeremiah?" Charlie asked.

"It's okay."

"Oh, no, you don't. I'm not going around all day feeling guilty about leaving you here hungry," Charlie said.

He turned the corner off Jackson Street and came to a jolting stop at the corner of Adams. He gave Jeremiah a five-dollar bill.

"You go into Annie's Cafe and have yourself a big breakfast on me."

"Five dollars for breakfast?" Jeremiah said. "I can eat all week on five dollars."

"You don't have to do this, Charlie," Nina said. "Jeremiah is very self-sufficient."

"I know that. He can give me change, if he wants. Come on, Jeremiah, do it as a favor."

Jeremiah took the bill and his mother opened the door and let him out. She planted a big kiss on his cheek.

"Oh, Mom!" Jeremiah said, his cheeks reddening.

He watched the truck until it turned the corner and disappeared.

Annie's Cafe was the only place in East Newport that was open twenty-four hours a day. It was in one of the oldest buildings in town, a wooden structure with a corrugated metal awning. Jeremiah thought it looked like a saloon in a frontier town.

A very bad sign painter had lettered the menu on the weathered siding outside the door. Jeremiah studied it and smiled when his eye fell on:

BeLgIaⴍ WAffLeƧ $1.95

The restaurant was jammed with the breakfast crowd, but Jeremiah found a seat at the end of the counter. He ordered Belgian waffles.

Some men at the table behind him were teasing their waitress about the size tip they should leave. He recognized the voices of Harry Sloan and the man he called Linebacker as they sat at the table.

Jeremiah huddled nearer the wall and hoped they wouldn't see him.

"What time should I bring the rotary mower down to start clearing out the brush along the creek?" Linebacker asked.

"I'll have to get rid of that big sycamore first. You can't get the big mower down there until it's gone," Sloan said.

"What do you figure, two . . . two and a half hours?" Linebacker asked.

"That may be rushing it. If I start as soon as we leave here, I should have it down by noon."

The waitress brought their breakfast. "I've got to get that place cleaned up by this time next week. Once I get a dozer down there, things will go a lot faster," Linebacker said.

"I'll call you if I get that tree down before noon," Sloan said. "That sycamore hangs way out over the creek. I can get it down, but I'll need help to winch the branches back to solid ground."

Jeremiah's spine tingled. He remembered his promise to Stacy that he wouldn't let them cut down their tree. They were both afraid that Charlie might not be able to stop these men in time. Their worst nightmare was happening this very morning.

Jeremiah quietly paid his bill and sneaked out of the cafe. He took off in a dead run for his house. *I have to have a plan*, he thought. By the time he opened the kitchen door, he had made up his mind. He ran to his room and snatched the handcuffs from the doorknob. He put his hands on the stair railings and slid down.

He jumped on his bike and headed for the Sink. He had ridden there so often that he knew exactly how long each leg of the trip took. It was seven minutes to Stacy's grandmother's beauty shop. He hoped that Sloan and Linebacker were still drinking coffee and telling jokes. It was another eight minutes to the old railroad bed, ten minutes more to the bridge. It would take a final five minutes to get to the sycamore. With a little luck, he could beat Sloan there.

Now he was glad he had taken Charlie up on breakfast. Not only did he find out about the danger to the Sink, he had the energy to do something about it.

Pedaling furiously, he estimated he was ahead of schedule by the time he saw Mrs. Hunter's shop. He saw Stacy picking up the newspaper from the porch. He slid to a stop.

"Stacy!" he shouted. "They're going to start cutting the trees in the Sink today. I'm going to stop them."

"Oh, no!" Stacy groaned. "Jeremiah, how on earth are you going to stop them?"

"I have a plan, but I've got to get there before Mr. Sloan does."

He didn't bother to wave. He popped a wheelie and took off in a spray of loose gravel.

He turned down the railroad bed. There were no signs of tracks in the grass besides those Charlie's truck had made earlier. The sun was much higher now. It beat down on him as he struggled down the rough path to the bridge.

He was relieved to see that Sloan's truck wasn't there. He slid his bike off the edge of the embankment and hid it under some thorny bushes. He stumbled down the incline and worked his way through the undergrowth. He was still gasping for breath as he looked back and saw Sloan's red truck stop near the bridge.

Jeremiah walked up the sycamore to his sitting place. He could see only the back of the truck through the leaves. He watched Sloan put down the tailgate and fill a large chainsaw with gasoline.

Sloan, chainsaw in one hand, gas can in the other, skidded down the embankment and out of sight into the brush. Jeremiah heard him pull the starter rope once, twice, three times. On the third pull, the saw sprang to life and the tops of saplings began to fall as Sloan cut a path toward Jeremiah.

More movement on the railroad bed caught Jeremiah's eye. Stacy had found his bike and stowed hers under the same bush. She sat on the ground and removed her shoes. She waded through the shallow lake out of sight of Sloan.

The chainsaw whined. More small trees toppled.

"Jeremiah," Stacy whispered. She was hiding in a stand of cat-tails at the base of the sycamore. "What do you think you're doing?"

"I'm going to stay up here. They won't cut down this tree if I'm in it. If they don't cut *this* tree, they can't move the heavy equipment in to clear the rest of the Sink."

"That's dumb, Jeremiah. They'll just make you come down."

"Shhh! Here he comes. Don't let him see you."

Harry Sloan walked into the clearing at the base of the sy-

camore. He put the saw down and wiped his face with a red ban-
danna. In the cattails, Stacy held her breath.

Sloan studied the base of the tree. Jeremiah thought he had seen
Stacy, but he hadn't. He bent over to pull the starter rope on the saw.

"Mr. Sloan?" Jeremiah called.

Sloan stood upright. He shielded his startled eyes from the
morning sun and stared up into the tree.

"What are you doing, kid? We told you to quit hanging around
here. You get down from there."

"I'm not coming down." Jeremiah said it softly, but defiantly.

"I don't want to have to come up and haul you out of there."

Jeremiah could see Stacy. She huddled close to the ground and
bit her lip.

"I'm staying up here until my mom and Charlie Willig come."

"Well, they better get here soon. I have orders to take this tree
out before noon."

"They won't be back by then, and I'm not coming down."

"You're on my son's baseball team, aren't you?"

"Uh huh."

"What's your name?"

"Jeremiah Stokely."

"Jeremiah, I'm going to ask you nicely one more time, then . . ."

"I'm not coming down."

Sloan put his hands on his hips and glared at Jeremiah. "We'll
see about that, kid."

Jeremiah thought Sloan was going to climb up the tree after
him, but instead he turned angrily and went back to his truck.

"Jeremiah," Stacy whispered. "You're going to get in a whole
lot of trouble."

"I don't care."

"They'll make you come down."

"I don't think so." Jeremiah grinned and pulled the handcuffs
out of his back pocket.

"Jeremiah, you're crazy. You wouldn't really handcuff yourself
to a tree, would you?"

"It depends."

They heard footsteps and Stacy went back to her hiding place.

"Well, now, kid," said Sloan. "We'll see how tough you really are. I got my boss on my cell phone and he'll be here in ten minutes. I suggest you get out of here before he comes. Mr. Franklin's not as nice as I am."

Jeremiah said nothing. He crossed his arms and leaned back comfortably on the limb. He glanced down at Stacy. She had her hands together like she was praying. "Jeremiah, please come down," her lips said silently. Her eyes pleaded, but he didn't move.

⌗ ⌗ ⌗

It may have been ten minutes, but it seemed like hours. Jeremiah saw another truck stop behind Sloan's. Linebacker came storming down the incline.

"What's going on here?" he demanded.

"Mr. Franklin," Sloan said, pointing at Jeremiah.

Franklin became furious. "Kid, I'm going to count to three. If you're not down by then, I'm coming up after you!"

Jeremiah didn't move.

"Okay, you had your chance. One!"

Jeremiah looked at the clouds.

"Two!"

Jeremiah ignored him.

"Three! That's it."

Franklin placed one foot on the base of the tree. His work shoes had slicker soles than Jeremiah's sneakers and his foot slipped. He caught himself and tried again.

"I wouldn't come up here if I were you," Jeremiah said. He dangled the handcuffs at arm's length.

Franklin stopped an instant, then started to climb again.

Jeremiah clamped his left wrist into the cuffs and threatened to hook the other end to a branch.

"You won't do that, kid. I'm calling your bluff," Franklin snarled.

He continued climbing. Jeremiah pulled the cuff around the branch and clicked it shut. He pulled a key from his pocket and dangled it over the water.

"He's not kidding," Sloan shouted.

Franklin, now within arm's reach, swung his hand toward the key just as Jeremiah dropped it. All of them watched the key fall, as if in slow motion. The key tumbled once, twice in the air and splashed into the water.

Franklin lost his balance trying to catch the key. He grabbed a small branch, but it pulled loose. He struggled for a new handhold, but it was too late. There was a splash as he slipped knee-deep into the creek.

"That kid's an idiot," Franklin said. "Come on. Let me use your phone. We'll see what the sheriff has to say about this." There was a loud slurping sound as he pulled his feet from the muddy bank. The men charged up the newly cleared path toward their trucks.

"Jeremiah," Stacy said. She came out of her hiding place to stretch her cramped legs. "That was the dumbest thing I ever saw. I can't believe you did that."

"I didn't have any choice. I'll stay here all night if I have to."

"Now you're up there for good. How will you go to the bathroom?"

"Stacy, pullease!"

"Gramby doesn't even know where I am. You're going to get both of us grounded until we're out of high school."

"I don't want to get you in trouble. Maybe you'd better go home. There's nothing you can do."

"I can't go home and leave you stranded."

"I don't think they'll really call the sheriff. They're just trying to scare me."

Stacy sat at the base of the tree and tied her shoes. "They're calling the sheriff, Jeremiah. They're not bluffing."

He saw Franklin and Sloan sitting on the tailgate of a truck. They were looking down the railroad bed as if they were waiting for someone. They didn't have long to wait. A police car stopped behind Sloan's truck.

"They called the sheriff, Stacy. They actually did it," Jeremiah said.

Stacy made it back to her hiding place just as the three men came into the clearing.

"What do you think you're doing, son?" a man in a brown uniform asked.

"My friend is trying to turn this place into a state park. I'm just trying to keep them from cutting down all the trees and ruining it."

"There are some things you've just got to accept, son," the officer said. He turned to Sloan. "What do you know about this kid?"

"His name is Jeremiah Stokely."

"Jeremiah," the officer said, "come on down; let's talk this over."

"He can't," Franklin said in disgust. "He dropped the key to the handcuffs into the creek. I'm going to get a bolt cutter and go up there and drag him down."

"Bad idea. That's the kind of thing that'll get you sued. What do you know about Jeremiah?"

"His mother's a check-out girl at Mason's," Sloan said.

"Well, then, let's get her down here, make her responsible," the officer said. They left.

"Stacy, did you hear that? They called my mom a 'girl.' How insulting."

"Insulting or not, she's going to be awful mad when she gets here."

"Nope. She's not at the store," Jeremiah grinned. "She went to Indianapolis with Charlie."

"Jeremiah, I've got to go. It's after nine o'clock and Gramby will be furious. I'll come back if I get a chance."

"After nine? Oh, no! I was supposed to be at the shop at nine-thirty."

"Good luck, Jeremiah." She waded back through the water to her bike. She looked back as Jeremiah gave a thumbs-up.

❖ ❖ ❖

The patch of shade that had cooled him earlier shrank. Jeremiah figured that by now they had discovered his mother wasn't at Mason's. He had counted on that to buy some time. There was no one else they could call.

"Bill," Jeremiah said suddenly. "The people at Mason's will tell them to call Bill."

Sweat stung his eyes. Shade bees flew around his face, seeking the salty moisture that collected on his forehead. The men on the railroad bed had taken refuge in the air-conditioned comfort of the sheriff's car.

As Jeremiah anticipated, Bill's van pulled in behind the other cars. The officer and Franklin talked to Bill for a moment, then all of them went down the slope to the creek.

"I have someone here who wants to talk to you," the officer said.

Bill walked to the base of the sycamore. Franklin stood behind him, smirking confidently.

Bill looked up at Jeremiah for a moment and said, "J.S., why are you up there?"

Jeremiah broke into a big smile. "Bill, why are you *not* up here?" he said. He used the same voice Bill used when he told the story about Henry David Something going to jail.

Bill smiled and turned to leave. Franklin's face fell. His smug grin gave way to a furious scowl.

"That's it?" he shouted at Bill. "That's all you're going to say to that brat?"

"That's it. The boy knows what he's doing," Bill said. He disappeared up the path.

The officer returned to the base of the tree, tilted his head back and squinted.

"Okay, Jeremiah Stokely. You won the first round. Let's see how tough you are when the sun gets hotter and the mosquitoes have chewed on you for a while." He motioned to the others and they returned to their air-conditioned vehicles to wait him out.

CHAPTER ELEVEN

Jeremiah's left leg had begun to cramp even before the men left. Now he was in constant pain. It was hard for him to move enough to keep his circulation going. Red welts were beginning to swell where the handcuffs chafed his wrist. The officer wasn't kidding about the mosquitoes. They swarmed around him and crawled into his eyes and nostrils.

He was beginning to doubt the wisdom of his wild plan. *Why am I doing this? I only started coming here because of Charlie. Now he and Mom are off somewhere having a good time, and I'm stuck up here all by myself. Even Bill and Stacy have deserted me.*

Now that the sun was higher, his shade was completely gone. The noontime heat bore down on the back of his neck. Tanned as he was, even with his cap turned around backwards, he could feel the sunburn. His nose felt fried, too.

He shifted to the other side of the limb to relieve his pain. All that did was put more strain on his wrist. His sweaty jeans clung to his legs. Then he noticed some movement on the embankment. Bill's van pulled in behind the lineup of cars and he was unloading something.

"What's he doing?" Jeremiah said aloud.

He unloaded the chalkboard he had given Jeremiah a long time ago. Bill leaned it against the van. With blue carpenter's chalk, he wrote in large numbers:

$975 ???

Binoculars dangled from a strap around Bill's neck. He raised them to watch Jeremiah's reaction.

"Yessss!" Jeremiah shouted. He gave Bill a thumbs-up.

Bill erased the numbers and wrote "SOLD!!!" He looked through the binoculars again. Jeremiah strained against the handcuffs and managed to get both hands above his head like a champion. If he had been on the ground, he would have been jumping up and down.

Bill put the chalkboard back in the van and drove away. The men on the hill watched him leave and looked at each other, puzzled.

"Yes! He sold my bookcase," Jeremiah shouted. His cry shattered the silence. It frightened a flock of red-winged blackbirds that had come to feed in the cattails where Stacy had hidden.

Jeremiah was so excited about Bill's good news that he didn't notice Stacy waving a Mason's grocery bag from the edge of the lake.

She rumpled the bag to get his attention. "Jeremiah, I brought some sandwiches," she said.

"You're a lifesaver, Stacy. Did you get in trouble for being here?"

"Not yet. But when Gramby finds out *why* we're here, look out."

She threw Jeremiah a stick with a string tied to it. The string was fastened to a plastic bag filled with food. Her first throw was off the mark. Jeremiah easily caught her second try.

Jeremiah opened the bag. It held two ham and cheese sandwiches and three chocolate chip cookies. In a separate piece of sandwich wrap, Stacy had sealed a tube of sun blocker.

"I hope it's not too late to keep me from frying, Stacy."

He awkwardly applied the ointment to his tender neck and his ears. After the initial pain of his touch, a cooling sensation came to the throbbing skin.

He unwrapped the sandwiches. "Thanks for the food, Stacy. I thought there might be a can of pop in here."

"Well, I was going to, but, you know—the bathroom."

"Will you get off that?"

She opened another plastic bag like the one she had sent up to Jeremiah. "I'll bet we won't forget *this* picnic for a while. Are you okay?"

"I'm glad you're back. I was beginning to think I had done the wrong thing. Can I ask you something?"

"Sure."

"When your dad first started dating your stepmother, how did you feel?"

"I hated it. I was so jealous you wouldn't believe. Why?"

"Mom wants to have a date with Charlie. I'm all mixed up. I like Charlie a lot. But I don't like him going out with Mom."

"I know how you feel. I thought was going to lose Dad."

"Did you?"

"Did I what?"

"Lose him?"

"No. We're closer than ever. The difference is that he's a lot happier. Before my stepmother came along, he used to sit up at night in the dark, just tapping a pencil on the table. I could hear it from my room."

"But my mom is happy. I take good care of her. I don't cause her any trouble. She doesn't *need* Charlie."

"You don't cause her any trouble? I suppose that when she gets home, she's going to say, 'Did you have a good day, Jeremiah? I mean, if you don't count being arrested by the sheriff.'" Stacy laughed.

"You know what I mean. She's always telling me how she appreciates me. I don't do any of the dumb stuff that some of her friends' kids do."

Stacy started to speak, but she and Jeremiah heard the noise at the same time. A fluttering sound came from the southeast. They looked at the island where Jeremiah supposed Spot still lived.

"What is it, Jeremiah? I can't see from down here."

"It's a helicopter. What the—"

The aircraft circled the old bridge and set down behind the sheriff's car. A cloud of dust enveloped the men on the embankment. They scattered, running for the safety of their cars.

"What's going on, Jeremiah? I still can't see."

"It's from a TV station."

"How did they find out about this?"

"Police radio, I bet. What do we do now?" Jeremiah said.

He twisted his arms around a big limb and watched as a TV

news team got out. The cameraman started taping as soon as the dust settled. Jeremiah could tell that the officer and Franklin were arguing with them. Franklin rushed the cameraman and put his hand over the lens.

"I wish I could hear what they're saying, Stacy."

"Jeremiah, this is killing me. What is going on?"

"I guess they want to come down here and take pictures of us, and Mr. Franklin doesn't want them to."

"Pictures of us? No way. Pictures of you, maybe."

Stacy darted from the cattails place and ran into the shallow water of the lake. She didn't even wait to take off her shoes and Jeremiah heard her splashing toward her bike.

"Coward," Jeremiah teased.

Jeremiah turned his attention back to the drama by the bridge. He hoped that Franklin would win the argument and keep the TV people from coming down the hill, but he lost this battle, too.

The cameraman came first. He turned the camera toward Jeremiah. A young blond woman in a red suit followed him to the base of the tree. She looked out of place in such a wilderness.

"Hello, up there," she said.

"Hello," Jeremiah said.

"I'd like to talk to you about why you're up in this tree. We'll take a few pictures if that's okay," she said.

"I don't think I better say anything. Everybody's already mad at me. I have to wait for my mother and Charlie to get here."

The officer whispered to her and she turned back to Jeremiah.

"A lot of people would like for you to come down. If you did, maybe we could talk then."

"I can't!" Jeremiah showed her the handcuffs.

"Oh, yes, the handcuffs. Well, if you don't want to talk, and you won't come down, I'll just have to talk to the people who *are* down here."

Jeremiah shrugged. The cameraman turned toward the woman.

"A drama is unfolding near East Newport," she began. "One that has County officials baffled. Early this morning, twelve-year-old Jeremiah Stokely handcuffed himself in a sycamore tree in a wetland southeast of town. Exactly why he did it, he won't say. All he will say is that he can't come down until his mother and a certain 'Charlie' get here. An officer from the Sheriff's Department has been here since early morning. Let's see if we can get some insight from him."

She turned to the officer. "This is Officer Sandburn of the County Police. Sir, why is young Stokely handcuffed to this tree?"

"Well, it's all a misunderstanding. It really isn't important enough for you folks to be making a big deal out of it," he said.

"But Jeremiah has been up there for several hours. Surely there is some explanation," she said.

Franklin broke into the conversation and the cameraman focused on him.

"He's up there because he's a brat. He's sick in the head. Been hanging around here for weeks, getting underfoot. We've chased him off several times," Franklin said.

"And you are?" she asked.

"Mel Franklin. My company has a contract to work here. This morning we were going to start clearing this area, but when we came to cut this tree so we can move our equipment in, there he was."

"Who is this 'Charlie' he's waiting for?"

"Charlie Willig from the Department of Natural Resources. He has some goofy plan to turn this stinking place into a park," Franklin told her.

"So there are plans to make this a park and—"

Franklin interrupted her. "There are no plans. It's just that state guy and this kid in the tree. He's been bringing bird houses here for weeks like he owns the place."

"It's just a misunderstanding," Sandburn said. "We'll have the problem solved in no time."

"But it sounds like you have a real stand-off here."

"Not really. Jeremiah will come down soon and everything will be back to normal," Sandburn said.

The young woman addressed the camera. "So there you have the essence of the conflict. Young Jeremiah Stokely is still up in the tree and the would-be tree cutters are waiting for him to come down so they can get on with their work. This is Jill Morrow, live from East Newport. We'll stay on the scene to keep you posted. Now back to the studio."

"You're off," the cameraman said. They turned to leave.

"You're going to be on the news, Jeremiah," the woman called out as she followed the cameraman up the path.

"See what you've done, Jeremiah? Now before you do any more damage, let me get Mr. Franklin's bolt cutters and get you down from there," Sandburn pleaded.

"When you get him down here, I'm going to teach him a lesson he'll never forget," Franklin said.

"Now, Mel," Sandburn said. "Come on. Let's go up on the hill and leave these *mosquitoes* to Jeremiah." He rolled his eyes at Jeremiah.

Jeremiah wished that he had his journal. *I need to write this all down before I forget it,* he thought.

"Jeremiah," Stacy whispered.

"Stacy, I thought you'd run out on me."

"I just hid until they left. I do have to go now. Gramby thinks we're having a picnic."

"Some picnic. Mom and Charlie ought to be here soon."

"How will your mom know where you are?"

"She thinks I've been at Bill's all day. She'll stop there."

"I'll come back if I can. I really hate this, Jeremiah." Stacy vanished into the brush.

Jeremiah's handcuffed wrist tingled. He massaged it with his free hand. He moved his left foot and slid painfully a few inches down the limb.

Oh, man, that hurts. If you think I'm doing this for you, Charlie Willig, you're wrong. If Mom hadn't taken the pictures and I hadn't promised Stacy to save our tree, I'd be playing ball right now, he thought.

A flock of swallows darted above the water, eating insects. "Go get 'em," he said. He looked at his reflection in Hog Creek. He felt alone until he saw two yellow butterflies chasing each other and a turtle crawl onto a half-submerged log. He saw a snake earlier but hadn't mentioned it to Stacy.

※ ※ ※

A TV van drove onto the embankment and parked behind the helicopter. A man climbed on top of the van and set up a satellite dish. The helicopter started its engine and, swooping over the Sink, it became a tiny dot in the sky.

Jeremiah heard car doors slam, then he saw Joseph Fowler walk around his red Jeep.

Joseph opened the passenger door. Stacy jumped out first, followed by her grandmother. "Mrs. Hunter," Jeremiah groaned. "She's going to kill me and make Stacy watch."

The three of them walked toward the bridge until Sandburn and Franklin stopped them. Mrs. Hunter stood nose to nose with Mr. Franklin, hands on her hips. She looked like a baseball manager arguing with an umpire. Jeremiah almost expected her to kick dust on Franklin's shoes anytime now.

The argument didn't last long. Mrs. Hunter won. Joseph helped her down the incline, and Stacy hurried ahead of them.

"I told Gramby what was going on, Jeremiah. She wanted to come down. Gramps wasn't home, so I asked Joseph to bring us," Stacy said.

"I told you I'd help you bring things here, Jeremiah. I thought I was talking about just bird houses. Are you okay, man?" Joseph asked.

Jeremiah nodded.

"Stacy told me what you've been doing out here," Mrs. Hunter said. Jeremiah braced himself for the worst. "I want you to know this is about the bravest thing I ever heard of."

Jeremiah sighed. "I thought you were coming here to jump all over me."

"No," Gramby said. "We came to keep you company until your mother gets here."

"You're a hero, Jeremiah," Joseph said. "You were on the noon news. They just interviewed Stacy. We're probably on TV right now."

Mrs. Hunter spread a blanket for them to sit on. She had brought dessert—pecan pie. Stacy put a slice in a plastic bag, tied it

to the string and threw the stick to Jeremiah.

"Do you have any idea when your mom will be here, Jeremiah?" Gramby asked.

"No, but I hope it's soon." He squirmed to find a position to sit in so it wouldn't hurt so much. There didn't seem to be any way to do it.

"I hope so, too," Joseph said. "Mrs. Loker invited a bunch of people to their house to watch you on the evening news. It would be too bad if you were still up there and we had to leave you to go to her party." Everyone laughed except Jeremiah.

◈ ◈ ◈

The sun had crossed the sky since he got to the Sink. Now it was hanging above the treetops in the west, casting its burning rays from yet another direction.

Harry Sloan had gone home long ago. Sandburn's shift was over and another officer had replaced him. Only Mel Franklin remained, pacing up and down at the top of the embankment.

Jeremiah saw the TV people sitting in the shade waiting for something to happen. Suddenly, a DNR truck rolled up in a cloud of dust.

"Mom's here," he shouted.

The TV crew jumped up and surrounded Nina and Charlie. Neither said a word. They hurried toward the bridge, down the embankment and to the sycamore.

Nina ran into the clearing. "Jeremiah, Jeremiah. What am I going to do with you?"

"Hi, Mom. Did we win?" he said.

"We won! The state okayed Charlie's proposal. We stopped at a restaurant after his meeting and we saw you on television. I should tan your hide!"

"But we won, Mom."

"I'll go get some tools to get you out of the handcuffs, partner," Charlie said. He was smiling from ear to ear.

"No problem. Watch this," Jeremiah said. He pinched the sides of the handcuffs and they sprang open. "Trick handcuffs."

"Jeremiah Stokely, you fake," Stacy shouted. "I'm so mad at you." She stamped her foot. "You could have gotten out of there any time."

"Yep," Jeremiah said proudly.

"But the key," Stacy said. "I saw you drop the key into the creek."

"That was the key to Bill's shop. He'll give me another one."

He slid down the tree, and the small group of radicals walked away. Jeremiah said nothing to the TV reporter, but the cameras were rolling as he lifted his bike into the back of Charlie's truck. He struggled into the cab beside his mother, rolled down the window, and waved a bug-bitten hand as they drove off.

CHAPTER TWELVE

He could hardly sit and the ride back to town was painful. Every bump made Jeremiah's muscles ache. His neck and shoulders were stiff. His nose and ears were blistered.

Nina broke the silence. "Jeremiah, that was a courageous thing you did, but it was also foolhardy. It worked out this time, but I don't want you to think you can go around taking things into your own hands. There are legal ways of doing things."

"I didn't want to do it, Mom. It was the only thing I could think of. You worked so hard taking pictures and Charlie wrote that proposal. I just had to do something."

"I know, Jeremiah," she said. She started to hug him but stopped. "When we get home, you soak in the tub. I'll put cream on your sunburn and you'll feel better. We'll talk then."

Charlie dropped them off at five-thirty. That gave Jeremiah an hour to work the pain out of his body before they were due at Ruth and Bill's.

"I have to let Rita know what happened," Charlie said. He lifted Jeremiah's bike to the sidewalk. "Did you know your saddlebag was torn, Jeremiah?"

Jeremiah looked at the damage. There was an oblong tear along the top and the zipper flapped. "Huh. Must have happened when I shoved it under the bushes," he said. "It's old anyway."

"See you in an hour or so," Charlie said as he drove away.

⬚ ⬚ ⬚

Jeremiah usually preferred a shower, but this time the steaming water, made frothy by Nina's bubble bath, invited him. He settled into the water, hoping it would soothe his agony.

He began to realize the seriousness of what he had done. *It could have gone either way*, he thought.

He turned on the cold water and soaked a wash cloth. He placed it on the back of his neck, hoping to draw out some of the searing heat. It helped a little. He slid down in the tub and rested his head on the edge. *Wait until Todd hears about this,* he thought.

His mother opened the door a crack and dropped clean clothes on the bathroom floor. The phone rang.

She came back to the door. "Jeremiah, can you dry off and come to the phone?"

Jeremiah pulled himself from the tub. His muscles felt better, but the water had made his sunburn hurt more than ever. He patted himself dry and saw in the mirror that his eyes were bloodshot, the left eyelid swollen.

He pulled on his jeans, groaning at the pain. He gingerly placed a towel around his shoulders and went to the phone.

"Jeremiah, I saw you on TV," said a familiar voice.

"Todd! I was just thinking about you. Don't you wish you were here?"

"See what happens? I leave you for a few weeks and you get in trouble. You wouldn't let me shave my head, and you go and handcuff yourself to a tree."

"You'd have done the same thing."

"I can't believe you did that, Jeremiah."

"I can't believe it either. I'd think I dreamed it if I didn't hurt so bad."

"They said there would be a special report tonight. I'll tape it for you."

"We're going over to Bill's to watch it. When are you coming down here to visit?" Jeremiah asked. He took the end of the towel and dried his hair, careful not to touch the burned skin on his neck.

"Mom may not let me if you're going to do dumb things like handcuff yourself in trees." Todd paused. "Just kidding. She thinks what you did was neat."

"We gotta get together," Jeremiah said. "But I have to hang up now. Mom is pointing at her watch. Maybe I can call you tomorrow or Sunday."

He hung up. "Todd saw me on TV, Mom."

"So he said. Come here and let me work on your sunburn."

Jeremiah winced as his mother attended to his wounds. She daubed cream on his nose and the back of his neck.

"Your left eye looks horrible, Jeremiah. I think it's insect bites, not sun."

"You can't believe how bad the mosquitoes were, Mom," he said. He tried to pat the sore place under his eye, but his mother pushed his hand away.

"That's the best I can do now. I'll look at it again before you go to bed. We really need to get over to Ruth's."

Jeremiah felt a little better. Joseph had said that there were a lot of people coming to watch the news.

"I kind of wish there weren't going to be a lot of people there, Mom."

"You're a celebrity. Don't let it go to your head, kid," his mother warned. She pointed her finger threateningly at him, then kissed her fingertip and pressed it on his forehead under the lock of blond hair where the skin had been protected from the sun.

Jeremiah put on his shirt. His mother had picked one of his softest shirts so his skin would not be more irritated.

They had just opened the back door when the phone rang again. "What now?" Nina said. She answered the phone.

"Yes, this is the Stokelys'."

She listened for a long time, then said, "He's right here. You'd better ask him."

She handed the phone to Jeremiah. "It's the TV station."

"Jeremiah," a female voice said. It was Jill, the TV lady. "We found your journal. You dropped it out there."

"I guess it fell out of my saddlebag," he explained.

"We'll return it, of course, but when we looked in it to see whose it was, we read what you had written about the sycamore tree. We'd like to read it on our special program tonight."

Jeremiah frowned. It was weird to think of anyone reading his journal. He especially didn't want anyone to read the letters he wrote to his dad.

"What part do you want to read?" he asked.

"We think you explained so well why you love the tree. Do you remember what you wrote about how old it might be?"

"I remember."

"We'd like to read just that part. Honest, Jeremiah, when we realized that you had written a lot of personal things in the journal, we stopped reading it. But that part was so good. We won't read it if you don't give us permission, but I think a lot of people would like to hear it."

"Maybe I should ask my mom."

"That's a good idea."

He cupped his hand over the phone. "They want to read something from my journal on the air," he said to Nina.

"I didn't even know you kept a journal, Jeremiah."

"It's just stuff I think about when I'm at the Sink. They said I don't have to let them read it if I don't want them to."

"What do you want to do?"

"I don't know. I guess it's okay if they just read the part about the sycamore tree."

"You do what you think is best. It isn't insulting to anyone, is it?"

"Oh, Mom. Of course not. It's just dumb stuff."

"If it's *dumb*, they wouldn't want to read it. Do you want me to talk to them?"

Jeremiah nodded and handed her the phone.

"Jeremiah isn't sure, so he asked me to decide. Would you read me the part you want to use?"

She listened as the passage was read to her. She smiled, "Yes," she said. "I think it would be fine for you to use that on your program."

Nina hung up the phone. "Jeremiah," she said softly, "that was absolutely beautiful."

⊡ ⊡ ⊡

Jeremiah almost always went to Bill's by going down the alley. This time, they walked down the street. The party was to be in what Ruth called the "front part" of the house. Jeremiah didn't go into that part often. The "front part" was the elegant old mansion that Bill had restored. The Lokers lived mainly in what had been the servants' quarters. It was where Jeremiah had spent much of his life.

A sizable crowd had collected at Ruth and Bill's by the time Jeremiah and Nina arrived. Jeremiah recognized the Fowler station wagon. Charlie's truck was parked across the street. Stacy, her grandfather and Gramby were walking up the front steps.

"Look, Mom. Ruth must have invited the whole town," Jeremiah said.

"It's a big event, Jeremiah. It isn't often that East Newport makes the news."

Ruth had decorated the parlor. She had tied balloons to the circular stairway. Blue and gold streamers stretched across the room. Bill had moved the television set from the family room and placed it near the stained glass windows. It was turned on with the volume down.

"Here comes our hero," Joseph said.

Everyone cheered. It felt like one of his fantasies, except he knew it was real. Ruth gave him and Nina some orange punch. Rita was sitting with Stacy in the window seat. Jeremiah joined them.

"Find a seat, everyone. The news is coming on," Ruth announced. They watched impatiently through the local news, the national and international news. Just before the commercial break, the announcer said, "Stay tuned for a report on the drama in a swamp near East Newport. That story when we come back."

Jeremiah fidgeted all through the commercials.

"Here it comes," Stacy said. She sat on the edge of her seat.

The program showed Charlie and Jeremiah lifting his bike into the truck on the embankment. Jeremiah peered at the screen and saw his journal on the ground by the rear wheel of the truck.

Jill Morrow's voice said, "The crisis in East Newport is over. About four-thirty this afternoon, twelve-year-old Jeremiah Stokely came down from a tree where he had spent the day. Jeremiah hand-cuffed himself in the tree to prevent the destruction of a wetland that is to become a state park."

The scene changed from the Sink to the studio. Jill was seated with the anchorman.

"Jill," he said, "you have been following this story all day. What really happened out there?"

"It's a fairly complicated story, but it's one that we think every-one will want to see. We spent the day in East Newport talking to people about the incident. We've put together a special report that we will air right after this program. It's a fascinating story about a boy, a tree and their friends. I hope all of you will join us then."

"Thank you, Jill. Now let's see what's happening on the sports scene."

Charlie brought in the park plans and Nina's pictures. He flat-tened the plans on the mahogany desk. Everyone gathered around as he went through a short version of his presentation.

He pointed to the location of the sycamore. "And here," he said, "is where Jeremiah spent a lot of time today."

"Charlie," Rita said, "don't you think they ought to name that tree after Jeremiah?"

"That's a great idea," Mr. Fowler said. Others agreed.

Jeremiah felt his skin turn even redder. Stacy smiled faintly as if she were suffering the embarrassment with him.

"It ought to be official," Rita said, "You know, like the Deam Oak up by Bluffton."

"The Stokely Sycamore," Joseph said. "It sounds good."

His mother came to his rescue. "Jeremiah may want to forget the whole thing. It'd be cruel to have a monument to keep remind-ing him."

"Thanks, Mom," he said. "Let me get you and Stacy some more punch."

Stacy sat in the window seat looking at Nina's photos. Jeremiah sat beside her. He realized it was the first time he had seen them.

"These are awesome, Jeremiah," Stacy said. "Look at this one of the leaves on our sycamore."

"I'll tell you a secret that only Bill and Todd know," he whispered.

Stacy leaned toward him.

"Mom took these pictures with a borrowed camera. I'm going to buy her a new one of her own."

Stacy started to say something, but Rita sat down beside them. Stacy smiled.

Jeremiah watched the TV out of the corner of his eye. The sportscast over, they went to the weather, another commercial, and back to the wrap-up. He would have been just as happy if Ruth had kept the TV muted but she didn't. As soon as "Special Report" scrolled across the screen, she hushed everyone and turned up the sound.

The show began with a wide shot of the Sink. It narrowed to a close-up of Jeremiah handcuffed to the tree. Background music swelled and the scene swung up to the sky, where a turkey vulture circled. The music was replaced by the sounds of the Sink—the chirp of crickets, the buzz of bees, the harsh call of a crow.

Over this scene, the narrator began. "In a time when there is concern about tropical rain forests and the health of our rivers and oceans, the story we are about to tell may seem insignificant. It's not, though. It's a story of courage and of being true to friends and to the natural world."

The scene changed back to the Sink. "In this small wetland in eastern Indiana, a story unfolded that is the essence of what's wrong and what's right in our thinking about wild places. Jill Morrow was on the scene when it all happened."

The screen showed the woman reporter standing in the clearing at the foot of the sycamore tree. "As the chainsaws roared," she said, "twelve-year-old Jeremiah Stokely handcuffed himself to this huge sycamore tree and refused to come down. Why he did it is not a simple story of defiance. It's a story that demonstrates urgency in preserving our wild places. Jeremiah didn't want to talk to us because he thought people were angry with him."

The scene changed from the Sink to the antique shop.

"Since Jeremiah wouldn't talk, we decided to talk to people who know him."

The TV showed the outside of Bill's shop, then the inside. The camera zoomed in on Bill. Across the bottom of the screen it said,

"Bill Loker, Antique Dealer."

"You know Jeremiah Stokely, don't you?" Jill asked.

"Yes, I know him. He's my business partner."

"You have a twelve-year-old business partner?"

"Sure. He's also my best friend."

"Do you know why he handcuffed himself in that tree?" she asked.

"Of course I do."

"They told us that you were contacted to talk Jeremiah down from the tree, but all you did was ask him why he was up there and then you just left."

"That's only partly true. It wasn't what I asked that was important, it was his answer."

"And what was that answer?"

"He said, 'Why are you *not* up here?' You see, to J.S., everyone who cares about wild places should have been up there with him."

"And why is that answer so important?" Jill asked.

"I've told Jeremiah the story of the night Thoreau spent in jail many times. When Ralph Waldo Emerson asked Thoreau why he was in there, he supposedly answered, 'Why are you *not* in here?' Jeremiah's answer was good enough for me."

"Mel Franklin, the man who is under contract to cut the trees, called Jeremiah a brat and said he was sick in the head."

"A brat? Hardly. Sick? The whole world should be as sick as J.S."

The scene faded to Jill standing in front of the County Building.

"That pretty much sums up one side of the controversy. Jeremiah knew that the state wanted to preserve the area—the Sink, as people here call it. But the county government had already commissioned a local contractor to clear the trees and dredge the stream."

Jill interviewed a member of the County Council who told her that it was usual practice for the county to contract with private businesses for such jobs. He claimed that he had only heard rumors, nothing definite, about plans for a state park. He said Mel Franklin was just doing what he was hired to do.

The scene changed to a close-up of Jeremiah's bird houses in the

Sink, then cut quickly to an interview with Rita.

"Yes, I know Jeremiah," she said. "I was with him in the Sink the day the idea came up about the bird houses. Our friend Charlie Willig told Jeremiah about his plans to turn the Sink into a park. He suggested that bird houses would encourage the return of Eastern bluebirds."

"Then you wouldn't call Jeremiah a brat, as Mr. Franklin did?" Jill asked.

"Jeremiah a brat? If he's a brat, I'm Big Bird," Rita laughed.

Then there was a close-up of Officer Sandburn.

"It's just a small misunderstanding," he said. "No laws were broken."

The camera then zoomed in on Franklin. Jill said, "This is Mr. Mel Franklin, who owns the landscaping company contracted to work in the swamp. Mr. Franklin, what can you tell us about the situation?"

"All I know is that I have a contract to cut the trees. When we got here, there he was—up in the tree."

"But if the state is going to turn this place into a park, cutting the trees would ruin it," Jill said.

"Look, I have a crew of people standing around here so we can do what we get paid for. It's not up to me to play politics."

"If the state takes over, won't they need to have landscaping work done?"

"I don't care who I work for. Until someone tells me different, I'm planning to clean up this place."

The camera came close to Jill Morrow. "We found out some other things about the standoff. Jeremiah told everyone that he couldn't come down from the tree until his mother, Nina Stokely, and Charles Willig, an officer for the Department of Natural Resources, got there. The two of them had gone to Indianapolis to submit final plans for saving the Sink. Mrs. Stokely is a photographer and her photos were a crucial element in Mr. Willig's convincing proposal."

The camera zoomed in on the yellow wildflowers blooming along the creek.

Jill continued, "Jeremiah realized that all their work—his mother's pictures, Charlie's plans, his bird houses—all would be lost if the trees were gone. "

Stacy's picture came on the screen. She was standing beside Joseph and Gramby, who was still frowning at Franklin. Along the bottom of the screen it said, "Stacy Hunter, Jeremiah's Friend."

"Stacy, how do you feel about Jeremiah being up in that tree?"

"It scares me," Stacy said.

"Do you know why he's there?"

"Sort of."

"What can you tell us?"

"I helped him bring bird houses down here. We sat up in that tree and watched the birds and talked about stuff. When the men chased us away and we knew they were going to cut down the tree, Jeremiah promised me he wouldn't let them."

"Did you know then what he was planning to do?"

"No, not until he did it. Even then I couldn't believe it."

"But you support Jeremiah's action?"

"He's my friend. He promised me he wouldn't let anyone cut our tree down and he kept his promise."

The picture cut to the councilman again.

"Certainly, if we had known of the state's plans, we would have cooperated. It's a matter of bad timing."

Then there was a shot of the Sink taken from the helicopter. It circled the area and focused on the sycamore tree.

"That was the situation this afternoon. What none of these people knew, not Jeremiah's friends, not his mother, certainly not the tree cutters, was that Jeremiah had been going to the Sink for weeks and keeping a journal of what he saw and heard and thought. We found the journal where he dropped it at the edge of the Sink, and we asked his permission to read one section about the sycamore tree in which he handcuffed himself."

The scene was in late afternoon, and the sycamore tree was silhouetted against the sun. Background music swelled, and Jill's voice resumed as scene after scene of the Sink passed before their eyes.

"The journal is difficult to read because, as Jeremiah points out, it is written the same way John J. Audubon wrote, both directions on the paper.

"Jeremiah writes:

I came to the Sink this morning just to sit in the sycamore tree. I can see a hawk not too far away. He can probably see me, too. I was wondering how long the tree has been here by the creek. Rita talks about seven generations. Maybe the tree isn't seven generations old, but I know of three. My grandfather came here. He may have climbed it and sat right here.

I know Bill came here when he was a boy, and now I come here and sometimes Stacy comes with me. It's an old tree and very crooked. It hangs out over the water, and sometimes ducks swim right under our feet.

This tree is the oldest living thing that I know personally. It makes a difference when you know something personally."

The screen changed to a closeup of Jeremiah getting into Charlie's truck. As the truck drove away, Jill said, "Maybe Jeremiah saved the tree because of Charlie Willig's plans. Maybe it was because his mother's pictures of the Sink were important to him. Maybe it was because he had promised a friend to protect the tree. Yet, it might have been something entirely different. It may have been simply because Jeremiah Stokely knew the tree personally."

The screen faded to black.

CHAPTER THIRTEEN

Jeremiah rolled over in bed and felt again the pain of yesterday's adventure. He put his hand on the back of his neck. It didn't hurt as much as it had, and the red stripe around his wrist was almost gone. He looked at the redwood sign propped against the side of his door. Last night, Bill had shown him the $975 check for the bookcase. Jeremiah couldn't believe someone would come all the way from Ohio to buy it. Bill had put the check into an envelope and pressed it into Jeremiah's hand.

The envelope had instructions printed boldly in Bill's distinctive handwriting. "Read the instructions and follow them," Bill had said.

Jeremiah had stuck it under his pillow before he went to sleep. His pain awakened him several times during the night. Each time, he checked to see if the envelope were still there.

He heard his mother coming up the stairs.

"I heard you stirring," she said. "How do you feel?"

"I'm a little stiff."

"Let me see that eye." She pushed back his hair. "It's still red. Not swollen like it was."

He scooted up in bed and looked into the mirror over his dresser. "I'll be all right."

"You are more than all right, sweetie." She picked up the wad of clothes where he had dropped them. "I'm going to work now. In all the excitement yesterday, I forgot to tell you that Mr. Mason wants me to take some pictures at the store. Better still, he's going to pay me."

"At the store? That's great, Mom."

"They're having a fifteen-year anniversary party tomorrow. When he heard about the pictures I took for Charlie, he asked me to take pictures at the party. That was before I knew the pictures from the Sink weren't any good."

"But the second ones were great."

"I hope my luck—and the blasted camera—hold out for one more day."

Jeremiah turned in bed and frowned with pain.

"Oh, hon. You're still hurting."

"It's not bad."

"I need to get going. Take it easy today. Do not—repeat—do not handcuff yourself in a tree. I'll be home about four-thirty." She planted a kiss on his forehead. "I'll bring ice cream and we'll have our own private celebration."

She left the room, humming a tune from the blues CD.

⊞ ⊞ ⊞

Jeremiah had a lot of things to get done. He pulled the envelope from under his pillow.

It said:

Step one: Go to the bank.

Step two: Start a savings account with half.

Step three: Start a checking account with the rest. Do you know how to write checks?

Your partner, Bill

P.S. I'd help you with this, but Ruth is taking me to the clinic for tests tomorrow.

He looked at the check again. He had never seen so much money, yet half of it wasn't enough to get the camera out of layaway. Now he had a new problem. His mother just *had* to have a good camera tomorrow.

He had already decided how to make up the difference. He found a brown Mason's grocery bag and swung it in the air. He grabbed his baseball card collection and stuck it in the bag.

He ate cereal, washed the bowl, picked up an apple and pedaled furiously to Arnold's Sports Shop.

Arnold was in the back room. He came to the showroom when he heard the door close.

"Well, well," Arnold said. "If it isn't East Newport's most famous citizen. What kind of trouble are you going to get into today, Jeremiah?"

"None, if I can help it," Jeremiah said quietly.

"Well, you certainly did your share yesterday. What can I do for you?"

"I want to sell my baseball card collection. How much will you give me?" He put the brown bag on the counter.

"Selling out? Are you sure you want to do that?"

"I'm sure. I've got some good cards."

Arnold flipped through the plastic pages of the notebook. Once in a while he turned back a page or two for a second look.

"I'll give you a hundred-fifty for it."

Jeremiah's heart sank. "I've got to have more than that. Look, there are whole bunches of Topps that haven't been opened. A couple of old ones."

"Yeah, I saw them. I guess I could go one-sixty-five."

"I checked them out with the Beckett price guide. They're worth at least two hundred," Jeremiah said. He tried to imagine how Bill would handle this.

"Have you been taking dickering lessons, Jeremiah? Okay, one-eighty. That's my final offer."

Arnold wrote a check and Jeremiah darted out of the store. The Second National Bank of East Newport was across the parking lot from Arnold's. Rather than go around the block, Jeremiah jumped the curb with his bike and slid to a halt by the automatic teller machine. He propped his bike against the guard rail and went into the bank.

He had been there before with Bill. It seemed a lot bigger and scarier now that he was alone. There were no other customers, so Jeremiah went directly to the first teller.

"What can I do for you?"

"I want to start two accounts, a savings account and a checking account."

"You'll need to see Mrs. Johnson," the teller said. She pointed to a desk in the corner. "She takes care of new accounts."

Mrs. Johnson looked up from her desk. She wore dark-rimmed glasses. Her unsmiling face was circled with glowing white hair, perfectly combed, not a wave out of place. She stared at Jeremiah.

"Yes?" she said coldly.

"I'm Jeremiah Stokely. I want to start two accounts."

"I know who you are. You were all over my TV last night and on the front page of the newspaper this morning."

"In the paper? I didn't see the morning paper."

"Well, you were there. You should be ashamed of yourself. Keeping those men from doing their jobs. It cost them a lot of money to spend the day fooling with you."

"I'm sorry, but all I want to do is start a savings account and a checking account."

"How old are you, Jeremiah?"

"Twelve."

"You'll have to have one of your parents present to start an account."

"But my mother is working, and I need to do this today."

"Your father?"

Jeremiah shook his head.

"Well, you can't start an account unless one of them signs for it with you."

"But Mom has to work all day. You close at noon on Saturdays."

"Well, you can call her. If she can get here before noon, we'll take care of it. Otherwise . . ." Mrs. Johnson said. She pushed her desk phone toward Jeremiah.

He squirmed in his chair. "I can't do that. I don't want her to know I'm starting this account." No sooner were the words out of his mouth than he realized how wrong they were.

"And, young man, that's exactly why we have this rule. We don't want you starting an account without your parents' knowledge."

"Well, will you cash a check for me?" He pushed the check for the bookcase toward her.

"This is an out-of-state check. We only cash out-of-state checks for people who have accounts with us."

"But I tried to start an account."

"When your mother comes in with you, and you have an account, we'll cash any check you want. Until then . . ."

Jeremiah's heart sank. "Bill Loker has an account here. I've been here with him lots of times. If he says it's okay to cash a check, will you do it?"

"If he takes responsibility for it, yes. He'd have to come here in person, though. A phone call won't work."

"Can I use your phone?"

She pushed the phone toward him and pretended to look busy with the stack of papers on her desk.

He let the phone ring seven times before he gave up.

"He's not home from the clinic yet. I'll just have to do something else."

"That's the rule, young man."

Jeremiah was confused, but he knew he had to get the camera out of layaway that day. He had waited too long. He couldn't let his mother take any more pictures with a camera that might mess up.

He pedaled to Phil's camera shop. Gilbert Paxon was stocking a glass-fronted refrigerator with film. He put down the carton of film and closed the glass door.

"Jeremiah, you're quite a celebrity. That was a crazy stunt you pulled yesterday."

"I know. I don't ever want to go through that again."

"What can I do for you?"

"I've been working with Bill Loker and I sold a bookcase. I have the money to get Mom's camera out of layaway."

"That must have been some bookcase."

"Roycroft. I got lucky."

"I have the camera in the back room," Gilbert said. He left the room. Jeremiah heard him talking to someone. Soon Jeremiah saw two smiling faces he didn't recognize peeking around the corner.

Gilbert came back with the camera in its box. He reached under the counter and brought out a brightly colored strap.

"I'll throw in the strap because you've been such a good customer," he said. He pulled a plastic bag from a rack and put the camera and the strap in. "How are you paying, Jeremiah? Cash or check?"

"Well, I have this check I got for the bookcase. Can I just give it to you?" He handed Gilbert the check.

"Wow. Nine hundred seventy-five dollars. You really got lucky."

"It'll be okay, then?"

Gilbert looked at the check again. His face became very solemn. "I'm afraid not, Jeremiah. We can't accept two-party checks."

"What does that mean?"

"It means that this check is written to you, not us. You're the second party. Phil won't let us do that. If you had a check written to us, there would be no problem."

"I tried to start a checking account, but they wouldn't let me."

"Why not?"

"They said my mother had to be with me. She's working, and anyway this whole thing is supposed to be a surprise. She doesn't know I'm getting her this camera."

"Bummer, Jeremiah."

"Gilbert, I've been working for this for nearly two years. Isn't there something you can do?"

"I'm afraid not. Phil would fire me if I took a two-party check this big, especially one from a different state. Work it out with your mother the first of the week and come back. I won't take the camera back to the storeroom. It'll be right here under the counter waiting for you. I'll even throw in six rolls of film for free."

"But, Gilbert, even if I can get Mom to help me get a bank account, she'll know how much money I have. She'll never let me spend it on her. Besides, Mom needs this camera tomorrow."

"Sorry, Jeremiah," Gilbert said. His eyes became very sad.

"I've lost," Jeremiah muttered. He put the check back into the envelope, clenched his fist around it and twisted his cap. Gilbert put the camera under the counter.

Jeremiah turned slowly to leave. As he reached for the brass handle of the heavy door, Gilbert said, "Jeremiah, wait a minute."

Jeremiah looked at him.

"Phil won't accept a two-party check from you, but I will. Come back and we'll figure this out."

Jeremiah hesitated. He was in no mood for another disappointment.

"You sign the check over to me. I'll write two checks, one to Phil for the camera and another to you for the difference."

"Will that get you in trouble?"

"Not if your nine hundred seventy-five dollar check is good. If it bounces, my wife will kill me."

"Why are you doing this?"

"You said your mom needs a camera tomorrow," Gilbert smiled. "Besides, I can't afford the time it takes to keep showing it to you. We're going to wear out the camera taking it out of the box."

"I'll do it if you're sure it's okay."

"You owe us six hundred thirty for the camera. I'll write a check to Phil for that amount. Then I'll write you another check for three hundred thirty-five dollars to make up the nine-seventy-five. That way, you won't have to carry around a bunch of cash until you get to the bank."

Jeremiah was so intent on what Gilbert was telling him that he hadn't seen Phil, the storeowner, standing behind Gilbert. Phil's face was very stern. Gilbert didn't know he was there either.

Jeremiah stood on one foot then the other as Gilbert finished the transaction.

Jeremiah put Gilbert's check in the envelope with Arnold's.

Gilbert put the camera in a bag and shoved it across the counter. "It's been a pleasure doing business with you, Jeremiah."

Jeremiah thanked him. He was anxious to leave before anything else went wrong. He opened the door and waved at Gilbert. He heard Phil say something about "tax." He didn't look back. He climbed on his bike. He was certain that Gilbert was in deep trouble. Jeremiah sneaked a glance back through the window as he rode away. Oddly, Phil was shaking Gilbert's hand and patting him on the back.

What is that all about? Jeremiah wondered.

CHAPTER FOURTEEN

Everywhere Jeremiah went, people stared. He stopped at the news stand and saw his picture on the front page of the paper. He thought about buying one, but he was certain his mom would pick one up at the store. She often got one if there were morning papers left when the evening papers got delivered.

He hadn't expected his errands to take so long, but with all the problems, it was almost noon by the time he returned home. He took the camera to his room and thought about how to wrap it. He imagined a beautiful package with a fancy bow and how excited his mother would be when she opened it.

"Nope," he said. "That's all wrong." He went to the kitchen and found another crumpled brown Mason's bag. He put the camera, the strap and the six rolls of film into the bag.

He scrounged around the kitchen for food. It was unusual that his mom hadn't left some lunch ready to pop into the microwave. Jeremiah guessed that with all the excitement, it had slipped her mind. He made a PBJ sandwich.

The phone rang. "How you feeling today?" Stacy asked.

"Okay. My nose and ears hurt and I've got a bruise on my behind from sitting on that limb."

"I got sunburned, too. Not as bad as you did, though. It was a nice party last night. Gramby asked Mrs. Loker for a copy of the tape."

"We don't have a VCR. I can watch it at Bill and Ruth's, though."

"I still can't believe it. You actually won."

"*We* won, Stacy. I couldn't have stayed there all day if it hadn't been for you and Bill. Gramby and Joseph were cool, too."

"And the next time we go there to sit in our tree, no one is going to chase us away."

"Let's do it next week."

"I can't. That's why I called. Shelly and I are going to visit Mama's parents for two weeks. I'll send you a card."

"Hey, I got Mom's camera."

"Awesome! How'd you get the money?"

"Bill sold my bookcase for me."

"I wish I could be there when you give it to her."

"I'll tell you all about it when you get home," Jeremiah said. "Have fun."

"You have fun, too. Don't get in any trouble until I get back."

"After you get back, it's okay if I get into trouble?"

"Silly."

Jeremiah wanted to call Todd long distance, but he thought he should wait until his mother got home. He cleaned up his lunch mess and took another look at the broken spring on the door. He found a pair of pliers and bent a new loop on the end of the spring. This made the spring an inch shorter and much stiffer. He swung the door open. It snapped shut with a resounding bang.

◆ ◆ ◆

The anticipation of his mother's return made the afternoon drag. At last, she came up the walk, carrying a newspaper and a sack of groceries. She opened the tightened screen door and knew at once that he had repaired it.

"I see you got around to fixing the door." Smiling, she handed him the paper and lowered the brown bag on the table.

"I already saw the paper. Pretty embarrassing, huh?"

"Not at all. I'm proud to know you, kid." She sagged down on the couch, shoved off her shoes without untying them, and heaved a huge sigh.

"Not everyone feels that way," he said, remembering chilly Mrs.

Johnson at the bank. "Want some tea?"

"I'd like that, Jeremiah. I brought ice cream for our celebration. Put it in the freezer, will you?"

He turned on the burner under the tea kettle. He had to rearrange the freezer to hold the ice cream. When the water boiled, he made his mother some herb tea, put the cup on a tray and took it to her. Her left arm hung limply over the end of the couch. She breathed deeply in an exhausted sleep.

He put the tray on the coffee table and quietly went to his room to wait for her to awaken. The time passed slowly.

It was nearly six-thirty when he heard his mother stir. He sneaked down the stairs and peeked into the living room to be certain that she was really awake. Jeremiah brought her the ugly paper bag.

"Oh, Jeremiah, I'm sorry. I promised we'd talk." She yawned and pulled her feet under her. "I was just so worn out. Don't be mad at me."

"No problem, Mom. Your tea got cold. Want me to heat it up?"

"No, that's okay. What's in the bag?"

"Oh, it's just some junk I picked up for you today."

He handed her the bag, just as he had planned it.

Nina pushed her dark hair from her face. She sat up straight on the couch and placed the bag on the floor between her feet.

"Let's see what you've got here," she said. She opened the bag and reached her hand in cautiously, as if expecting a prank. First she pulled out the strap. Her eyes widened in wonder. "What is this for, Jeremiah?"

"Take the rest of it out of the bag, will you? But don't drop it."

She pulled out the camera box. She looked at it a full thirty seconds before she could speak.

"Jeremiah, how on earth?"

"It's all yours. And it's paid for. Honest."

Her heart pounded. Struggling to open the box, she withdrew the camera and stared at it in disbelief.

"It's beautiful! I don't know how you did it, sweetheart, but tell me, and we'll see if we can keep it."

"I'm telling you, Mom, it's yours."

Jeremiah told her the story, starting with putting the camera in layaway when he thought he could pay for it with mowing money. He told her about the bookcase, the trouble at the bank, and about Gilbert helping out. He didn't tell her about selling his baseball cards to make up the difference.

"I just had to get your dream back, Mom." He sat down beside her.

"Oh, Jeremiah, you did all that? Is it any wonder I'm so proud of you? You know I can't let you do this. We'll have to take it back. You should be saving your money."

"You can keep it, Mom. I have answers for all your arguments. Too expensive? Nope. I have money left. Mom, I've worked nearly two years to get this. Don't make me take it back."

"Let's look at the camera. We'll decide later."

They studied the camera, figured out every lever and button. They looked at everything in the room through the viewfinder and read the owner's manual from front to back. They stopped only long enough to get some ice cream and read it again.

It was stuffy in the living room. Nina put the camera back in the box, and they went out on the back porch. The stars had never hung more brightly over East Newport. They seemed so close they could have been touched with a yardstick.

Jeremiah dangled his legs off the porch and looked toward the silhouette of the horse chestnut tree. His mother went inside for a moment and then returned with something in her hand.

"Just look at those stars, hon." She sat on the step beside her son. "Thanks for working so hard to bring back my dream." She paused a moment. "I think it's only right for me to give you back yours."

"What do you mean, Mom?"

"I picked this out of the trash." She handed him the beat-up brown envelope that the Postal Service could not deliver to his dad. "I know that this holds your dreams. I just couldn't let you throw them away."

He had thrown the package into the trash, sat under the horse chestnut, and tried to convince himself that there were no buffalo—

that he couldn't count on his dreams. Now, the cellophane tape on the envelope reflected the starlight. Fireflies danced through the grass of the vacant lot. A cicada launched its song on the night air and into his dreams.

They stood in waist-high prairie grass. His mother's brand new Nikon rested on a sturdy tripod, focused on bulging shadows on a distant hill.

"Jeremiah, what a good idea. I'd have never thought of taking pictures of buffalo at night," Nina said. She looked at her famous naturalist son as he studied the lay of the land to determine the best shots.

"You'll have to take a timed exposure, Mom. There's only starlight. I bet the fireflies will make interesting streaks in your pictures."

"You're right, Jeremiah. The fireflies are starting to come out. 'Buffalo by Starlight and Fireflies.' What a good idea for a photo essay."

The sounds of the night surrounded them. They sat close to each other, waiting—waiting in the middle of a buffalo herd in Oklahoma.

"I bought the fastest film Gilbert had. With good equipment and your talent, I know you can do it, Mom."

"Steady the tripod, hon. Hold fast."

"Hold fast, Jeremiah," Nina said again.

"What did you say, Mom?" The Oklahoma prairie vanished. The lowing of the distant herd was replaced by the hum of cicadas.

"I said, 'Hold fast to your dreams, Jeremiah Stokely.'"

She hugged him, and he tightened his grip on the brown envelope.